Kale is a Four-Letter Word

ISBN: 978-1-951122-09-6 (Paperback)
ISBN: 978-1-951122-14-0 (ebook)

LCCN: 2020933083
Copyright © 2020 by Corrales Writing Group, LLC
Cover Design: Alexz Uría
(facebook.com/dandeliondesignmx and
alexzuriaphoto.com)

Printed in the United States of America.

Artemesia Publishing, LLC
9 Mockingbird Hill Rd
Tijeras, New Mexico 87059
www.apbooks.net
info@artemesiapublishing.com

Kale is a Four-Letter Word

An Anthology by The Corrales Writing Group, LLC
and guest contributors

Edited by Patricia Walkow and Chris Allen

**Artemesia
Publishing**

Other Corrales Writing Group, LLC Publications

Love, Sweet to Spicy
Love, Sweet to Spicy in Color
Passages
Passages in Color
Currents
Corrales Writing Group 2014 Anthology
Corrales Writing Group 2013 Anthology

Corrales Writing Group Members

Chris Allen
Maureen Cooke
Sandi Hoover
Jim Tritten
Patricia Walkow

Guest Contributors

Jane Butel
Sandi Cathcart
Adrienne Evatt
Jasmine Tritten
Walter Walkow

Illustrations and Photos

Illustrations and photographs are credited at the end of
this volume, in order of appearance.

Contents

Contents by Author

Recipes

Jane Butel   *Slivered Kale Salad with Roasted Winter Vegetables and Spicy Orange Sesame Dressing*

Sandi Cathcart   *Colcannon*

Sandi Hoover   *Kiki's Kale Salad*
                     Surprise Green Smoothie

Adrienne Evatt   *Adrienne's Kale Pie*

Jim Tritten   *Kale des ordures – a "Down the Hatch" Kale Recipe*

Introduction

Finding a nutrition-focused magazine or newspaper article that does not deify kale is impossible. Somehow, this particular cultivar of *Brassica oleracea* has become the darling of the superfood world.

For now.

At some point it will pass its radiant divinity to some other vegetable newly identified as a god by whoever makes, or thinks they make, these decisions for the rest of us.

Not that we care.

Unfortunately for kale, some of us either secretly or blatantly despise this particular branch of the cabbage family. We find its taste foul and its texture repugnant. If you are one of these people, this book is for you.

"Oh, but I love kale," you say.

My condolences.

Yet, this book is for you, too—if you have a well-developed sense of humor and are open to a new perspective on kale.

Some stories are about wives urging their spouses to eat the so-called healthy vegetable, however objectionable it may be. Others are horror stories about kale. We have charming illustrations, great photos, quotes about kale, and a host of suggestions for using this particular vegetable in a non-traditional way.

We even have some recipes…kind of. Maybe.

Enjoy our anthology's irreverent look at all things kale. It's time to fire this plant's publicist.

Patricia Walkow, Editor

Project Resurrect and Illuminate Kale (PRIK) team at work in the conference room.

Keep Kale Cool

Chris Allen

Bella Hart, General Manager of Produce Magic, LLC, knew the name flashing on caller-ID. "Damn." She tweaked her face into a smile and picked up the receiver. "Good morning, Cameron. How's it blooming?"

"I am not happy, Bella." Cameron Nash was Chief Produce Officer of Amalgamated Foodgroups, Inc. and Bella's biggest client. "I just thumbed through last quarter's sales report. Kale has slipped in the superfood standings. Again. There's an increase in anti-kale memes on social media, and someone published a report that kale is potentially toxic. Probably some grad student scrambling for an original research project, but shit!"

"OK, Cameron, calm down. I'll get my staff together and we'll create a revised kale marketing plan."

"I want something in my inbox by five o'clock this afternoon. And Bella...."

"Yes?"

"It'd better be good. I got kale coming out of my...."

Hitting the disconnect button before Cameron could finish, Bella called her best ad people to a brainstorming meeting. "You know the drill, folks," she said to the twelve people sitting around the conference table. "We've got an angry client, and we need to boost his product. Let's hear your ideas."

The first person to speak was Eric, a slender, pasty-looking fellow in a pin-striped suit. "We could rice it. You know, like cauliflower."

"Gees, Eric, that's stupid," Rose responded. "Kale doesn't have the same body as cauliflower. It's a leaf."

"How about kale pizza crust?"

"And just how would you make that? Kale turns a slimy dark green when cooked. Do you think that would be appetizing?" Ginger asked.

Bonnie jumped up and down in her seat. "How about using it to fill underwear pads, you know, like for leaky old people? Dried up, it could be superabsorbent, and old people represent a huge demographic."

"Yuck!" Harvey slunk back in his chair. "That is just disgusting."

Four hours and six gallons of lukewarm spinach smoothies later, the team had a plan. Since he was the first to speak, Eric was forced to take the lead on Project Resurrect and Illuminate Kale, otherwise known as PRIK.

"Cameron's going to love it." At least, Bella hoped so. "Daily progress memos on where you are with kale, Eric. We have to turn this waxy bastard around before it's too late."

Note: All PRIK memos appearing throughout this book are written by Chris Allen. The author would like to thank fellow writer John Atkins for his contributions to this story and the memos.

4

Project Resurrect and Illuminate Kale – Memo 1

TO: Bella
FROM: Eric
RE: PRIK, Week 1

PRIK is off to a good start. The following initiatives are underway:

• Team Chemistry is scouring the planet for at least one chemist who would be willing to go on the record and defend our marketing department's suggested benefits of kale. The intent is to highlight only the positive—superfood due to dense concentration of organic material. Keep it vague. No flatulence references.

• Team Kale Light is working up a storyboard to push the use of kale powder in candle making. It may not do anything, but if we spin it right, doomsday fanatics will fill their bunkers with the stuff in order to keep their off-the-grid lights burning at night. No word from R&D about carcinogenic properties.

• Team Kale Light also is developing a vape prototype—Kale Inhale. Long shot, but worth taking.

That's the current list. Ideas continue to pour in…trickle in. Bonnie is checking with farmers about how much we have to unload immediately before the next quarter numbers are released. More later.

Eric

Creamed kale? How bad can it be?

The Kale Virgin

Patricia Walkow

"**W**hat's this?" Walt asked me.

He held up a clear plastic bag from our favorite meal kit delivery service.

"It's kale."

"Kale?"

"Yes…the recipe says we are going to make creamed kale with our steak tonight."

He raised his eyebrows. "It'll probably be like creamed spinach, don't you think?"

Shrugging my shoulders, I knew better, but remained silent. I didn't want to prejudice his imminent experience with kale that wasn't so disguised he would actually know what he was eating. It would be his first time.

Half an hour later we sat down to a visually attractive meal of creamed kale, sirloin steak, and roasted potatoes. Walt dipped his fork into his green vegetable, stuffed the morsel in his mouth, and abruptly stopped chewing. His eyes widened.

I looked at him. "What's wrong?"

He swallowed hard and reached for his glass of water. "It's not spinach."

"I know. It's kale."

"It's supposed to taste like spinach."

"No, it isn't. It's OK. Just eat it."

"I can't," he whined. "It's thick, like leather." He slipped his fork under it, as though expecting to find something. "And it's slippery. Gross. I'm not eating it."

"I use kale in soups quite often. You eat it."

"It isn't bad when it's chopped in bits and tastes like chicken soup. Here I can see it really IS kale. And I can taste it, too." He pushed the offending greenery to the far side of his plate. Unable to abide its presence any longer, he got up and tossed the repulsive vegetable down the disposal.

"What about cabbage?" I asked. "Cabbage and kale are in the same family. You love stuffed cabbage. You've driven cross-town sixteen miles each way for a plate of it."

"Don't even compare them. That's a sacrilege."

"Sometimes you eat red cabbage. No complaints. How about roasted Brussel sprouts...you eat them, don't you? They're in the cabbage family, too."

"I don't really like them that much. Smothered in balsamic vinegar and a bit of brown sugar, I'll eat them. But I HATE kale. I now understand why so many people can't stand it."

"You mean you hate kale when it tastes like kale and you can see what it is?" I teased.

"Yup. Do you like it?"

"It's edible," I replied, "but wouldn't be my first choice for a green, leafy vegetable."

Kale now joined his list of toxic vegetables. It was preceded by asparagus—the vegetable he hates most. When he sees it, he reacts like a vampire seeing a cross; then it was okra's mucilaginous pods, which are edible only when fried to a crisp and no longer slimy, followed by starchy plantains that he thought should taste sweet, like bananas.

That left us with string beans, peas, a few types of lettuce, and spinach as acceptable greens.

I put my fork down. "You know, kale is an interesting food."

"I don't care," he responded.

"It's packed with an amazing amount of nutrients. Its cultivation has been traced to the eastern Mediterranean as long ago as 2,000 B.C. It's ancient."

"Yeah...it tastes it," he snarked at me. "Why didn't they just keep it there?"

"Its arrival in the West, actually Canada, can be attributed—or blamed—on the Russians. 1800s trappers, I think."

"So, it's their fault I had to taste this crap."

"Stop acting so silly," I said.

"It's crap. Utter crap."

"Did you know a botanist named David Fairchild championed it and spread it south?"

"Yeah, so it could sully the pristine, once-kale-free expanse of America the Beautiful."

"It's a very attractive plant, too," I offered, "and can grow under many conditions. That makes it a survivalist's dream."

"Yeah," he said, "and my nightmare. I bet it couldn't be annihilated by a hydrogen bomb."

As we finished supper, I thought of other so-called trendy "superfoods" identified by sallow-hued, thin-skinned vegetarian nutritionists with sunken eyes, and magazine editors who need content. Kale joined the ranks of blueberries, beets, sweet potatoes, and pomegranates as near-perfect food sources. Yet, it has none of their pleasant qualities. Somehow, its countenance is on magazine covers all over the U.S.

Much of it is super-hype. Within twelve months another vegetable long eaten by humanity will be magically identified as a "new" miracle food...just because the current crop of food mavens has had a revelation. These are the food experts and trendsetters who enjoy telling the rest of us what we should eat. I tend to take anything they say lightly, except for dark chocolate. That's a great superfood.

And tomorrow night I will try to expand Walt's palate's universe: artichokes.

He told me he doesn't understand artichokes because the way I prepare them you don't actually eat them but scrape the "meat" off the leaves with your teeth. Yet properly trimmed, steamed, stuffed with butter and breadcrumbs, then briefly baked, he may enjoy the taste, if not the texture. That is, it won't taste like an artichoke, but like crispy, buttery crumbs.

But I expect he will add artichokes to the list of vegetables that will never touch his lips again.

That's OK because it's only a matter of time before the food fashionistas discover artichokes, making the vegetable ooh-so-cool and more overpriced than it is now.

It saddens me that kale isn't outrageously overpriced. I'd have a better reason to ignore it.

My husband would agree.

Project Resurrect and Illuminate Kale – Memo 2

TO: Bella
FROM: Eric
RE: PRIK, Week 2

PRIK continues. Here's today's update:

- Team Powder recruited an office worker who likes to cook. She took a sample home to try making kale-based pizza crust. She is optimistic about the results and will report back tomorrow.

- Team Powder is also exploring a marketing concept referred to as Project Kalpers—Cheaper than Pampers® and good for the environment. All we need is a few babies or maybe old people. Below is a conceptual image with a kale design element:

- Team Powder is, in addition, investigating the use of crushed kale as a building material. Concrete, bricks, drywall. The team is most excited to try it as an ingredient in adobe bricks. A team member suggested that adobe uses mud, crap, and straw. Kale's got to be as good a choice as any of those things.

Feedback from Week 1: Team Kale Light hit a snag. The Kale Inhale prototype kind of exploded. Just a little. The good news is the test subject has sworn off smoking.

Eric

The Ultimate Vegetable: Part 1

Jasmine Tritten and Jim Tritten

While driving through Northern California on a trip, I heard Jim's stomach growl. From experience, it meant stopping at the nearest restaurant to fill his primal needs. So, we pulled into a more-than-decent-looking roadhouse and sat down for lunch. As I opened the menu, the salad section hit my face right away. I pointed my finger to one particular item.

"Jim, look at the picture of this salad. It's got some of your favorite ingredients. Crispy bacon. How can *you* go wrong with bacon? Toasted pears, sweet tomatoes, and creamy avocado. Even Boursin cheese with caramelized onions. Wow, it looks incredible. Besides, it will be so good for you."

Jim grabbed the menu, "Let me look."

Oh no. Here she goes again. She omitted some of the salad ingredients. Doesn't she remember last time I fell for hidden components in a salad? Nice restaurant with pleasant company for lunch. I asked the son of our lunch companion what he recommended—he worked there. He suggested the "Asian Fusion" salad with ahi tuna. The tuna was rare, not at all fishy, and practically melted on the tongue. A bushel of jade-colored leaves was hidden under the tuna. I figured OK; I'll get my monthly quota of greens with this one meal.

So, I shoved in a large mouthful and was immediately struck by the difference in the quality of the chew. When I bite into lettuce or spinach, it tears, then disintegrates into smaller pieces, and has a taste matching the dressing. With this stuff, it had a rubbery consistency. More like wax. Remember those tiny wax Coke bottles we got as kids? Felt about the same in my mouth. You can grind it between your molars for a very long time and when you are done, the stuff is still largely intact.

But the flavor on my tongue is what overwhelmed my senses. This elastic green substance had the taste of insect repellent. It's not like I swig insect repellent. But face it, when you lather your body with insect repellent, or bug-spray your head and extremities, you can't help but inhale some into your olfactory system. Ugh—terrible stuff. Why would anyone want to eat something that tastes like insect repellent?

Ten minutes later I was still chewing. Ten minutes after, I searched for a paper napkin to receive the macerated wads of green. I asked the son what I was eating. "Kale" was his response. Never heard of it—but a name to never be forgotten. I left the rest of the bushel of kale in the bowl without taking another bite. I burned the word "kale" into my hard drive memory so I would never repeat the mistake. So why would Jasmine think I would even consider eating another salad with kale? Hasn't she seen my postings on Facebook? Didn't she hear me tell this story at least a dozen times over the past year? How am I going to extricate myself from this predicament? Perhaps if I try something like, "Interesting. I'd love to try it, but my doctor told me to cut down on fatty foods like creamy avocado.

"How about I have a turkey sandwich instead?"

Obsessed by Kale

Chris Allen

Sebastian stomped his boots on the mat, littering it with gray slush. "Cold as hell out there, even for Minneapolis!" he grumbled, shrugging off his parka. His nose caught a whiff of something divine. Kitty must be cooking an incredible meal this evening, he thought. He detected simmering chicken, onions, and peppers. There was a hint of something else, but a cloud of spicy scents wafting through the hallway quickly masked it.

He headed to the stove and wrapped his arms around his wife. Then he pulled back her thick black hair and nuzzled the nape of her neck. "How did I manage to find a woman like you?"

Kitty was the head of marketing for a meal prep company. Her hobbies included gourmet cooking coupled with an appreciation of fine liquor. It was a mystery how she cooked such spectacular meals and still kept him fit and healthy.

Kitty laughed. "Go set the table, lover boy. It's almost ready."

A few minutes later, Sebastian leaned over and gazed into a bowl, admiring its contents. "God, this looks delicious." He sampled a spoonful, savoring the spices that danced on his tongue. Then he frowned. *Wait, that can't be right.* He examined the dish again. Strands of wilted green leaves floated among the chunks of meat and vegetables. Sebastian put his spoon down. "Kitty," he said, his voice low and his head bowed. "There is something I have to tell you. I should have told you before we were married."

Kitty paused, her spoon midway to her mouth. An unwanted image jolted through her mind. A perky blonde played in a sandbox with a toddler that resembled Sebastian. Her left hand tightened around her napkin. "What is it, Sebastian? What should you have told me?"

He stared into her cobalt blue eyes, noting they had grown brighter. "I hate kale."

"What? Is that it? You hate kale?"

Kitty's laughter sparkled like popping champagne bubbles. "Oh, my god! I thought you were going to tell me you had a mistress and a child stashed somewhere. You silly goose."

"It's just you love to cook."

"Yes, and kale is a superfood, loaded with antioxidants, fiber, and Omega 3. It's so good for you. But, if you hate it, I won't cook with it."

"Are you OK with that?" He reached out and touched her hand.

"Of course. My brother John hates turnips, and he's told Maggie he would divorce her if he so much as smells turnips cooking. I want to stay married to you, babe, so out goes the kale." She stood and reached for his bowl. "I'll freeze this for my lunches. Go order us a pizza, and sweetheart, load it with cheese and pepperoni."

Sebastian raised his glass of wine in a toast to his magnificent wife.

Kitty adored her husband. He was witty, ambitious, and his body had the toned muscles of a professional athlete. A lock of blond hair curled above dark-brown eyes flecked with hazel. He was a successful entrepreneur who designed an app that alerted people to hidden allergens in food products. He and Kitty were rising socially, committed to various nonprofit causes. Soon they would start their long-delayed family. The man she loved had few vices: a tendency to play too many video games, smoke expensive cigars, and now, a dislike of a cruciferous vegetable.

The kale thing remained a private joke between the two of them until they attended a charity ball for the arts. As they passed through the buffet line, Sebastian stopped in front of an elevated chafing dish. "Kale with shallots and garlic! No. No. No. I paid $150 a plate for this. No self-respecting charity would serve that."

Kitty flushed red and shrunk behind his shoulders. *What was he thinking to raise such a fuss over a vegetable at such a prominent event?*

Several friends there that evening heard about Sebastian's aversion to kale. His relationship with the vegetable became a running joke, rampant across social media. His friends tweeted when they ate kale, posted pictures of kale dishes, and created memes they sent to Sebastian's website. He would counter by posting anti-kale memes, such as showing the benefits of ordering kale with a silent "k," or showing someone trying to make kale chips who ends up drying the leaves into a crumbly, dusty gray-green heap.

One afternoon, Kitty strolled through the antique district on her way home. In a shop window she spotted an oil painting propped on an easel. The tag said the title of the painting was *Kale Friend*. The lower part was a field thick with dark green and purple crinkled leaves. Above was a turquoise sky. In the center stood a round, dark blue-bodied creature with a small pale blue head from which sprouted golden horns. Its eyes sparkled.

Kitty stepped inside the shop and asked the proprietor if she could look at the piece. When she examined it, she noted black printing in the lower left-hand corner. It read, "I've been waiting for you in the kale."

"Perfect!" Kitty chuckled. "My husband is in a war with his friends over that vegetable. This is the perfect anniversary gift for him. I'll take it!"

On October 22, five years after their wedding day, they sat on a patio at Le Boeuf overlooking the river that ran through the city. An attentive waiter arranged their entrees on the table and then poured each of them a glass of white wine. Sebastian tasted his sausage and white bean cassoulet. Then he pushed it away, the knife and fork clattering. He sat back in his chair and sighed. "I take you to the best restaurant in Minneapolis, and I get kale in my cassoulet."

Kitty stared at him. She adjusted the shoulder strap of her red and black dress. She had taken extra care to look lovely since it was such a special occasion. Now Sebastian threatened to throw a shadow across the evening.

"Here," she said, picking up her plate. "You eat mine and I'll eat yours. There isn't any kale in Tuscan shrimp."

"Are you sure you want to switch, babe? I can order something else."

"Of course, I'm sure. I love you, and I don't want to ruin this special night."

"It's just..." Sebastian shuddered. "I can't understand how anyone can eat it."

After finishing their dinner, they headed to their townhouse overlooking Stone Arch Bridge. The lights of the city twinkled as the couple grasped each other, their passion increasing as they kissed. Sebastian lifted Kitty up and headed for the bedroom. "Wait!" Kitty teased. "I have a gift for you."

"Better than this?" Sebastian grunted as he hefted Kitty further into his arms.

"It's a small thing, but I'd like to give it to you now." Kitty laughed. She hoped this artwork would be the highlight of Sebastian's adventures with kale.

"Where is it?" He gently placed Kitty back on the couch. She bounced up and ran for the gift, gloriously wrapped in silver foil and hidden in the hall closet.

Sebastian ripped open the paper to reveal the kale creature surrounded by a sleek gold frame. He read the caption, "I've been waiting for you here in the kale," and roared with laughter. "It's perfect, my darling. I love it! Tomorrow we'll hang it in a place of honor in my office."

Over the next few months, Sebastian expanded his participation in the kale melee, but what began as a joke soon became an obsession. He talked about the risks of kale consumption at every opportunity, how some animals shunned kale, and how certain studies debunked the vegetable's health benefits. He modified his top-selling app to warn consumers of products that contained kale.

The joke was now running on marathon time.

"Superfood, my foot!" he would exclaim. "That odious vegetable doesn't deserve to grow on this planet. Slimy and evil-tasting, even cooking it with bacon cannot redeem that terrible plant."

As Sebastian worked, he would gaze at the picture Kitty gave him. He admired the swirls of color the artist used to create the beast. The vivid shimmering eyes were almost hypnotic. *Metallic paint? What made those eyes so lively?* One day, as he passed by the piece, he noted its expression. *Did it always have that furrowed brow?*

One afternoon as Sebastian passed by the painting, he heard the creature growl. When he told Kitty about it, she responded, "Babe, you're taking this a little too far. I'm worried about you."

He ignored Kitty's concern and immersed himself in his business. Every day he would scan through social media for more posts slamming kale which he would repost with glee. He began a blog to expose restaurants that dared to serve the dreaded green leaves. He acquired a large following among those who had tired of people preaching the political correctness of eating kale and other superfoods. He even launched a popular line of clothing with anti-kale slogans.

On a brilliant morning in March, he entered his office and opened the curtains. Snow was melting, crocuses peeped through the ground, sun streamed onto his desk. As he stared out the floor-to-ceiling windows at the floating ice chunks on the river, he called to his sound system to shuffle some soft jazz.

A moist arm grabbed him around the throat and dragged him backwards.

"What the…!" Sebastian called out, his arms clawing at the pressure around his neck.

A breathy, musky voice whispered into his ear, "You have it wrong, sir."

Sebastian thrust his shoulders forward trying to throw his attacker.

His assailant moved with him and then yanked him upright again.

"I will prove it to you," the voice whispered again, expelling an odor that reeked of damp compost. "You will love it."

Sebastian twisted to the left where he felt a weak point in the perpetrator's grasp. As he spun his head, he detected one eye behind him, a yellow, glittering eye. Then something wrenched his head forward again.

"You cannot get away. You are mine. You will see. You will see…" the voice rumbled.

A quick stab in his neck, and something warm wetted the collar of his shirt. *Why are the windows dancing?* The whitewashed ceiling came into view as he was thrust onto the floor. A face, was it a face? A light blue blob with golden horns churned above him. It merged into a swirling gray palette; then the gray morphed into blackness.

When Kitty arrived home later that day, Sebastian did not respond to her call. She toured through the rooms, repeating, "Hey, babe? Where are you?"

When she opened his office door, she gasped. The furniture was in disarray, her anniversary gift, *Kale Friend*, had been knocked onto the floor, and next to it, there was a disheveled pile of her husband's clothes, the collar and shoulder of the shirt soaked with blood.

The investigators never found a body, never saw evidence of an intruder, and could never determine how an intruder accessed their apartment. Nor could they define a motive for the attack.

Kitty and all of Sebastian's known contacts had solid alibis, and the security cameras did not record any images of strangers. His disappearance remained unsolved.

Devastated by her loss, she never remarried, never had children, and upon her death, an executor distributed her estate among her siblings' families.

The painting, *Kale Friend*, did not appeal to anyone else and was sold at her estate sale, eventually traveling from one second-hand shop to another.

"Mr. Shapiro?" The well-dressed young man hesitated at the open door of the art appraiser's gallery. "Is anyone here?"

"Yes, come on in. I was getting a cup of tea in back. What can I do for you?"

"My name is Eric. I found this interesting painting in a junk shop, and a friend suggested you might be able to tell me more about it."

"I can certainly try," Mr. Shapiro said.

Eric placed a paper bundle on the counter and un-wrapped it to reveal the picture framed in gold.

Mr. Shapiro lifted the piece and placed it on the carpet-ed counter. "I know this painting," he mumbled. "Yes," he said, slapping his hand on the counter. "I remember now." Looking back at Eric, he explained. "A long time ago, a woman brought this in, and I appraised it. It stuck in my memory because a few months later, her husband disappeared. So tragic. It was all over the news."

Eric ran his hand down the edge of the frame. "I bought it to give to my wife who abhors kale. I thought it would be a funny joke. Can you tell me anything about it? When it was painted? Who the artist is?"

Tapping his finger on the counter, Mr. Shapiro thought for a moment. "I believe I may have something in my files that can help us. Back then I took careful notes. I was at the beginning of my career, you see. I'll be right back."

Eric could hear Mr. Shapiro as he shifted boxes and slammed cupboard doors. Then, the shop owner re-appeared, brushing dust off a large three-ring binder. Placing the binder next to the painting, he flipped to the relevant page. "See, I even took a photo. It was such an intriguing painting. No artist signature, just a caption in the lower corner."

Adjusting his glasses, the old man bent over the piece, mere inches from the surface. "Yes, yes. This does appear to be the same painting. Wait. Something's off. I don't think that's the same writing." He read from the binder, "There is a caption that reads, 'I've been waiting for you here in the kale.'" He returned to Eric's piece. "This one says, 'I have you in the kale.' How odd."

"Hm," Eric said, focusing on the notebook. "You're right. The captions are different." Looking again at the painting, he asked, "What about those dots in the background? Is that damage that's occurred over time? It appears the paint has flecked away."

"Where?"

Eric pointed to the blemishes—small points which lacked the vivid green and purple of the leaves.

"Hang on." Mr. Shapiro rifled through a drawer and brought out a jeweler's loupe. Bending within millimeters of the glass, he gasped and staggered backward. Dropping the loupe, he cried, "That's impossible!"

Eric picked up the loupe and scanned that area of the painting until the dots came into view. Bringing the loupe closer to the surface, Eric watched as they resolved into the bodies of people. One, a naked man, gaunt and gray, blood streaming from his neck, thrashed among the leaves.

He was screaming.

Eric impulsively leaned in, placing his ear against the glass. He heard a faint, raspy sound. "…are prisoners, and all we have to eat is goddamned kale!"

Obsessed by Kale was previously published as *Obsession* in *SouthWest Writers 2019 Writing Contest Winners Anthology.*

Project Resurrect and Illuminate Kale – Memo 3

TO: Bella
FROM: Eric
RE: PRIK, Week 3

This is turning out to be more challenging than we antici-pated:

- Team Powder is pushing the envelope. They explored a kale-seaweed cleansing masque for the cosmetic market. One team member mixed powdered kale and seaweed with a little cosmetic mud and applied it to her face, but she fell asleep. Her dermatologist thinks the green tint should fade in a month or two. Here's what she looked like and this idea is now off the table:

- Team Chemistry's report is not positive. Chemists re-fuse to engage. The team leader will reach out to third-rate community colleges or trade schools looking for funding. If we front them enough money, their students might come up with something. Kale, the new semiconductor?

- Team Health is pursuing a kale suppository. Given the slimy nature of stewed kale, it should be an easy sell in the over-the-counter constipation relief market. They are having a hard time finding a willing volunteer to give it a try. Plus, the prototype suppository is about the size of a Twinkie.™ Still working on it.

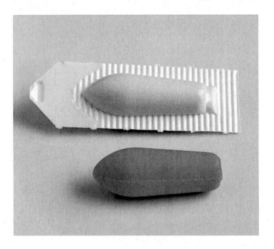

- Team Powder's pizza crust experiment didn't go as planned. When kale powder comes in contact with water, it turns into a slimy goo, even when mixed with lots of flour. The office worker was vehement. There's not enough pepperoni in the world to make it edible. Also, she decided it was time to do a kitchen remodel and start eating out more often.

Eric

The Ultimate Vegetable – Part 2

Jasmine Tritten and Jim Tritten

At home in our kitchen one morning I gave my husband Jim a tall glass filled with a smoothie made by my Blendtec® 3-horsepower blender—the one with the four-inch surgical steel blades rotating at 300 miles per hour.

"Try it, darling. It's super delicious made with almond milk, banana, non-fat Greek yogurt, and some frozen pineapple pieces."

Jim took a sip of the healthy-looking concoction, lifted his head with a frown on his face and stared at the glass, "What's the green color from?"

"I also added some kale to give it more flavor and nutritional value," I answered.

Oh no, not again. What is it about women? They always want to improve men. I was doing just fine for the past five or six decades until Jasmine got this blender. Now every time I turn around, I'm handed a glass filled with various types of fruit and vegetables, and I'm told how good it will be for me. How come what is right for me never seems to taste good? I mean almond milk is OK if you purchase the variety mixed with coconut milk or chocolate. Besides if I'm going to ingest yogurt, why low-fat? And who said the Greeks know anything about yogurt? I know it is appropriate as an addition to main courses. But low-fat yogurt? I mean the Greeks are the same people who drink retsina and call it wine. Retsina is right up there with kale as something one should never, ever put into one's mouth. So how in the hell am I going to get out of this situation? Possibly if I try something like, "Interesting. I'd love to try it, but my doctor told me I can't eat pineapple—bad reaction with one of the drugs I take. How about I have a turkey sandwich instead?"

Lips that have touched kale will never touch mine.

---Jim Tritten

The Dark Side of Kale

Walter Walkow

Kale is touted as one of the most nutritious foods on the planet—a superfood. But what do we truly know about kale? It was already in use as a food source in the Eastern Mediterranean before Rome knew about it. They referred to it as "caulis." It made its way throughout the rest of Europe somewhere around the 13th century, and hundreds of years later it was introduced to the west.

But this is not the complete story.

When kale is referred to as one of the healthiest foods on Earth, the reference to "on Earth" is not accurate. Kale originated beyond this planet. Actually, beyond our own Milky Way galaxy. In fact, kale was brought to Earth by the Kaliens, a species of extra-terrestrials. They used it as a vehicle to plant (no pun intended) a chemical in humans, which would be passed onto future generations via genetic drift (I have no idea what that is, but it sounds impressive). In large concentrations in a human host, the chemical causes intense emotional distress, severe aggression, and an uncontrolled desire to purchase sale items at Christmas time. The objective was that one day in Earth's future, when enough humans were infected, the implanted chemical would be triggered. Then, the humans would riot against each other, thus destroying much of the world's population, making invasion easy.

The aliens' early tests indicated fully-kaleated humans would display a deep green tint on their corneas accompanied by a strong odor of rotting food, though the latter only occurred with exceptionally high consumption of the plant. At various times throughout the ages, the crafty Kaliens tested kale's growing effect on humans and attempted to determine how widespread it had become.

The first test occurred in Rome about the 15th of March, 44 BC, known today as the Ides of March, the day Julius Caesar was assassinated. Historians have attributed his murder to disgruntled Roman Senators, but in truth, kale was responsible. Once the chemical was activated by the Kaliens, senators with high concentrations of caulis instantly became violent and descended on the unsuspecting Julius. Caesar noticed a strange green tint in the eyes of the approaching senators and recognized a familiar foul smell permeating the area. As the assassins began their vicious attack, Caesar cried out *"Et tu caulis?"* Bleeding on the ground, he moaned "Why? Why?" Even the senators who did not participate in the attack bore the strange green tint in their eyes and were heard shouting, "Kale Caesar! Kale Caesar!" For centuries historians have misquoted them.

The Kaliens were encouraged by the success of caulis, but were disappointed in the limited spread on Earth. So, for the following few thousand years, additional Kaliens were transported to help proliferate the crop throughout Europe, Asia, Africa, and North America. They even altered the crop by adding more nutrients, hoping to appeal to the health conscious, and therefore increase its use around the world.

The next test occurred over 1800 years later. By then, the conniving Kaliens introduced kale to much of Europe, especially England and France. They were eager to evaluate the effect of the chemical on a large population. They chose 1789 France because much of the farmland was covered with the prolific vegetable. Plus, the food was so much better than England. The ruddy vegetable even had the support of the Queen, Marie Antoinette. When asked what the common people should do when there was a severe bread shortage, she immediately announced "Let them eat kale."

And so, they did. Mass quantities were consumed, whereupon the anxious invaders activated the chemical and then waited. It didn't take long. French peasants rioted, and on July 14, 1789, they stormed the Bastille, which coincidently started the French Revolution. Unfortunately, some of the Kaliens were caught in the chaos and suffered the same fate as Marie and lost their heads. The remaining Kaliens left, vowing never to come back to France no matter how good the food and wine.

The final test was in 1947 at a small town in New Mexico called Roswell. The chemical was activated but there seemed to be little change in human behavior. Kalien scientists surmised the caulis concentrations were too low, and humans were developing a level of immunity to it.

They tried to increase the concentrations by direct contact with the population, and while that did produce some agitation in the populace, it did not last. The scientists were frantic and experimented with new doses by treating the plant's water source. However, they did not realize that was also their own water source and inadvertently injected themselves. Without the same immune systems as humans, they began to succumb to the chemical. Once they realized what occurred, the inept invaders attempted to return to their galaxy for treatment.

However, they became aggressive and violent with each other, causing some of their space craft to crash with numerous fatalities. The bodies and some space craft material were recovered by the U.S. Government.

Soon the Kalien bodies became disfigured and turned the same green color as kale. Eventually, each body withered into a clump of wilted, rotting vegetation.

The invaders who managed to return to their galaxy infected so much of their own world that they abandoned their quest for an Earth invasion. They had to struggle to avoid extinction as the population was decimated by rampaging inhabitants.

So how do I know so much about the dark side of kale?

Just look into my eyes.

Project Resurrect and Illuminate Kale – Memo 4

TO: Bella
FROM: Eric
RE: PRIK, Week 4

The teams are working their butts off. Sorry about the over-run on the budget line item for cocaine-based coffee. These guys deserve it.

- Team Attire came up with a terrific idea. Designer bikinis. They wove fresh kale leaves into tops and thongs. They looked spectacular. We rounded up some test subjects and sent them out to the beach. Unfortunately, after several hours lying in the sun, the leaves dried up and blew away. Marjorie, Nikki, and Roma were transported to the hospital where they are recovering from second-degree burns. I'm sure they each have personal insurance to cover the cost. On the bright side, Josie came up with a brilliant save. We could infuse the bikinis with sunscreen and market them as "Intro to Nude Beach Bathing Suits— Arrive covered, leave naked." I think this could really put kale on the map.

- Team Accessories has explored using kale in the manu-facture of scarves. It turns out compressing kale leaves under 10,000 pounds of pressure will turn it into a du-rable fabric. However, it is stiff as a board. Our first test subject wearing the scarf tried to exit through a door and took out the door frame. Recognizing most people want to wrap scarves around their necks, the team is hopeful it will find a solution.

I remain optimistic.

Eric

Not even the compost pile wants kale.

Give it an Inch

Sandi Hoover

One spring afternoon, William Mallon found a worn leather pouch tucked between field rocks in his garden wall. The stiff material resisted his tugs, but he finally got it open and poured the contents into his hand. His head swiveled suspiciously, as if the person who had left them might suddenly appear and accuse him of stealing. *Just a bunch of tiny seeds. Will they grow? Wonder what they'll be.* He relaxed when, as usual, he did not see a soul in any direction. He thought perhaps a friend had left them as a joke.

But there was no one there to surprise him.

A loner, Mallon was confirmed in his bachelor status and liked his remote location. He had a large garden plot, merely feet from his kitchen door. That planting area had been hard-wrested from the rock-filled soil, now outlined by walls created from those same rocks. He took great pride in the quality and quantity of vegetables he harvested each year. Sturdy greenery was flourishing in neat rows, promising another fulfilling year.

Past his garden, his solitary house faced a slope dropping to a walled-off goat pen. Beyond was more pasture with black-faced sheep lying contented in deep clover, then a cliff edge with sea beyond. Below the cliff, out of sight, was his small boat, waiting for his frequent quick fishing jaunts to provide himself dinner.

But he had enough empty space at the back of his garden to plant another vegetable. He tossed the small seeds as he walked through the open area and stomped some dirt over them. *Old seeds, like their rotten bag. If they come up, fine, if not, fine, since I'm through planting this season.*

Almost daily, when not out fishing, he walked through his garden with hoe in hand and removed any weed having the effrontery to ruin the pristine nature of his plot. The exception was off in the corner. Green sprouts had appeared, but he didn't bother weeding the unknown seed's space. He wasn't sure what the new plants would look like and he hadn't been careful to put the seeds in rows. Whatever the green thing turned out to be, William could always feed the vegetable to his goats if it grew. *I'm sure my goats will eat it, weeds or not.*

As days passed, the green sprouts grew larger. *Those crinkled leaves are fancy, but I still don't recognize them. I'll leave 'em 'till they look big enough to eat. I'll take a few to my friend George, who knows all about plants.* He cut a couple to carry with him when he next went to town.

George gave his considered opinion the plant was some sort of kale, but a variety he had never seen before.

"Kale's reputed to be highly beneficial and healthy, but not high on the preferred list of vegetables."

Several days later, Mallon was looking across his garden, to the far edge. Plants he recognized in the strange patch were waving to and fro when nothing else showed movement. Shriveling and shrinking as he watched, they were dying. He saw the kale, as George called it, had grown around their base. *Are those leaves choking them? Are they eating the weeds? Whatever they're doing, it's helping me, so good for them.*

As days passed, Mallon's appreciation turned to concern as the plants spread. He took his hoe and went one evening on his normal rounds after missing days due to shearing sheep. He was startled to discover the unknown plant had crept into his veggie garden and was strangling a cabbage.

"I can't have this. You have to go!" William exclaimed, as he hacked with his hoe at the offending leaves. They were tough to cut, but with repeated swings he succeeded in separating the aggressive leaves from the rest of the deeply ruffled, blue-green bush.

Is it my imagination, or is it changing color? I'm sure it has gotten darker since I first hit it. He pulled the chopped-off leaves into a heap at the foot of the wall. Satisfied he had stopped the plant by pruning its encroaching leaves, Mallon puttered around the rest of the garden for a few more minutes. He left after picking some beans and lettuce to accompany his evening meal.

When he approached his garden the following afternoon, hoe in hand and machete on his hip, he had a shock. The kale had once again covered the original cabbage. It also overran one whole row of cabbages and enveloped a third of the frilled carrots. The supposedly dead leaves at the wall had become a sturdy vine, tendrils overtopping the rocks and several arms weav-

41

ing in the air searching for higher support. "Aah, the pruning efforts to contain this plant haven't worked. It's growing faster than before. I'll have to uproot the whole thing."

At his feet, a rumpled blue-green leaf was leaning toward his boot. He stomped on it without thinking. "Back off! What kind of plant does this?" Mallon smacked it with his hoe.

The kale responded. Its leaves stood straighter, unfurling to their full size and waving back and forth. Disconcerted, he stepped back from the plant and tripped over the mounded row of leeks. Scrambling to his feet, "It must be my imagination—it can't be moving toward me. Oh, yes, it is!" He pulled out his machete and whacked off the closest vines. They writhed and curled into tight spirals. Mallon speared them with the point of the machete and tossed them over the nearest wall.

Overnight the plant and its leaves grew larger, with tougher stems. Daily he hacked the greenery back. He'd started carrying his axe and throwing the leaves over his rock wall onto the hardpan road. Those sprouted and crawled up the wall from the outside. He threw some in the pen with the goats. They took one bite, shuddered, and spat out what they were chewing. They backed away from the pile and William watched as the leaves wriggled and pushed themselves into the soil.

When he counted his goats the next morning, one was missing, and kale in the pen covered more than half the space. *Suppose? No, plants can't make a goat disappear overnight. He must have been a bolter, but how?*

He went to town and bought weed killer. It might as well have been fertilizer. The kale absorbed it, growing faster and larger after the spraying. Its fierce liveliness made the plant too frightening to eat.

"What do I have to do to stop this malevolent thing?

It has covered, no, devoured all the vegetables, and if I didn't know better, I'd say it's headed for my house."

That night Mallon slept restlessly, certain he was hearing the plant creeping closer. In the early morn, he stepped outside and stopped in shock. "Holy mother, it wasn't my imagination. Those leaves can't be more than twenty feet from my door."

He stood in front of his tool shed, hoping for some brilliant insight to stop the plant and save his property and the remnant of his garden. The large can of kerosene caught his eye. *This'll do it in.* The contents sloshed as he carried the can to the closest part of the kale patch. Kale was no longer simply overflowing the small area at the back of the garden. It was a green wave, overrunning and consuming the domesticated vegetables. Mallon drenched the nearest leaves and watched for a reaction.

It was instantaneous. Leaves at his feet turned magenta and spread to their full width. There followed a wave of color pulsing from the closer plants to the far end of the property buried by the kale. The ground vibrated and William felt a pressure in his chest as if there had been close thunder. At the far end of the kale-covered garden, the plant blackened, and the ebony shade rolled toward him. He threw the rest of the kerosene as far and wide as possible. He backed away from the groping edge of the kale, and whirling around like a discus thrower, sent the empty can spinning to the far end of the field. Leaves curled toward it from all sides and buried it in a mound of green.

William thought to run, but not before he tossed a match on the kerosene-soaked kale. He smiled as the flame soared momentarily. His face fell as the flame faltered, died, and aside from a wisp of smoke, left no evidence of having happened. "What?! Die dreadful plant!"

Once more he felt as if someone were pressing on his chest. He lurched down the path. He saw the kale had spread across the pen and had the frightened goats cornered. He opened the gate to the goat yard. "OK, boys. You're on your own. Good luck." They nearly knocked him down in their frenzy to abandon the kale-filled pen. Bleating frantically, they scattered downhill and leapt over the low wall adjoining the trail.

"Damn!" He stumbled on the steep rock-strewn path, and almost fell. William shouted at the placid faces watching him from the pasture. "Sheep, beware the kale. You get your freedom too." Unmoved, their heads bent again to the grass they were cropping.

At the cove where his small runabout was upturned on the shingle, he righted his boat, pushed it into the shallows, and mounted its outboard motor. He stowed his gas can under the aft seat. With an escape route at hand, William took a moment to look up the slope. "No, that's not possible!" His home was ablaze. A maroon sea of leaves was pulsating around it, spilling over walls and across paddocks. "I...I need to warn someone."

Brilliant purple dazzled his eyes when he managed a last glimpse of his property. "I'll tell George. He saw the first leaves and identified them. He'll understand."

Intent on his heading, William didn't notice the small leaf caught in the tread of his shoe.

Project Resurrect and Illuminate Kale – Memo 5

TO: Bella
FROM: Eric
RE: PRIK, Week 5

As a reward for working so hard, I ordered kale salads for everyone. No one was able to stay to partake. Do you know any pig farmers who would like twenty pounds of kale salad?

Progress so far:

- Team Military met with several generals from the Pentagon. The team pitched the idea of a kale cannon to spray oncoming troops with liquified kale powder. Called Kale Defense. The generals loved the concept. Upon being struck with Kale Defense, troops would instantly grimace at the bitter taste, rendering them completely incapacitated. Eyes burning, olfactory senses triggering a vomit response, the enemy becomes easy fodder (pun intended) for capture. The downside is nobody can stand to be near them until the smell wears off, estimated to be six to eight weeks.

- Team Uniform was completely engaged in devising a way to use kale for camouflage on helmets and uniforms. Unfortunately, they became disheartened when they heard of the bikini failure and left the office. I found them later in a pub plastered on whiskey and kale chips.

As you know, government contracts and weapons development can be quite lucrative. I am convinced this is the best path to success. You know the military. Call it a weapon and they'll buy it.

Eric

The Ultimate Vegetable – Part 3

Jasmine Tritten and Jim Tritten

During a dining experience at a friend's house, they served soup as a first course. Viewing the culinary treat, Jim and I sat down at the nicely decorated table. After leaning forward over the silky-looking substance, I inhaled the aroma through my nostrils and with a smile said, "It smells divine. What kind of soup is this?"

Our hostess turned her head in our direction, "This is a smooth, earthy, rich cauliflower-kale soup made with extra virgin cold-pressed olive oil, Purplette Onions, organic celery stalks, Inchelium Red Softneck Garlic cloves, chicken broth made from scratch from range-free chickens, and more herbs than I can remember."

Jim's face turned dark green, and I saw him scowl.

Oh no, here we are again. Sneaking kale into soup. All the rest of the ingredients sound edible. But kale? No. Can't spit it into a paper napkin. Nothing in there I can blame on the doctors. Can't ask for a turkey sandwich instead.

After the last episode, I did some research on kale. Apparently, kale has a wax that alters its texture, making it difficult to chew. The wax is a defensive mechanism making the plant unattractive to herbivores. So, will a kale soup coat my stomach? I also learned kale incorporates silica into its cell walls, something about making it compression-resistant. I have first-hand knowledge about strong cell walls from the Asian Fusion salad episode. But had no idea about the silica — thought it was only an output from Intel into our air. I'll bet the hostess first beat the kale into submission with her own Blendtec® 3-horsepower blender with four-inch surgical steel blades rotating at 300 miles per hour.

Think man, think...wait, maybe this will work: "The soup looks positively divine. What a terrific smell. I'm sure it will be simply delicious. Let me take a spoonful....Oww," as I cupped my hand over my mouth.

"What is it?" our hostess asked.

"My tooth broke off."

"From soup?" Jasmine asked.

"Not directly from the hot soup. I had a temporary crown installed this morning, and the heat must have loosened the new bit, so the top part came off. I think I swallowed it! Excuse me; let me go check myself in the bathroom mirror. I'll just skip the soup for now."

Project Resurrect and Illuminate Kale – Memo 6

TO: Bella
FROM: Eric
RE: PRIK, Week 6

The PRIK continues. Here's today's update:

- Team Floral has been consulting with wedding planners. They all agreed kale's use in that setting could be expanded. The planners were excited about the frilly appearance and color range of the leaves. One of the planners had a wedding the following day and incorporated kale into the bride's bouquet. Here's a photo:

Regrettably, turns out the bride had a previously unknown allergy to kale. Halfway down the aisle, she began to sneeze uncontrollably and collapsed. The groom has threatened to sue, so, for the moment, that planner has no interest in obtaining large quantities of kale.

I still think PRIK has a chance to be successful. We continue to explore the possibilities.

Eric

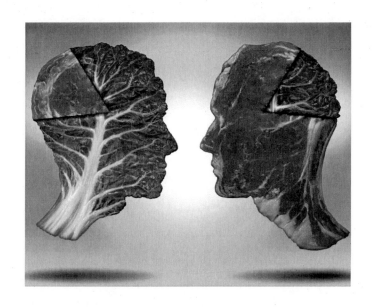

It's Only Because I Love You
A Comedy

Maureen Cooke

Cast of Characters

Paul Chambers

A bit paunchy
50ish Male

Janelle Chambers

Trim
40ish Female

LIGHTS UP; ON JANELLE AND PAUL CHAMBERS' living room. The room is modestly furnished: couch, chairs, coffee table. No TV. Artwork hangs on the walls. It is an open room adjacent to the kitchen.

JANELLE CHAMBERS is mid-40s. She is athletic, dressed in running shorts. Throughout the play, she does quad stretches, lunges, and the like.

PAUL CHAMBERS is late 40s/early 50s. He has the look of an aging football player, not particularly trim, but not fat. He wears a Hawaiian shirt and cargo shorts. Throughout the play he sits, occasionally pats his pockets, as if searching for something.

The play opens mid-conversation.

JANELLE
What I don't understand, Paul, is why you couldn't have just told me. I mean, what's the big deal? So, you don't like kale.

PAUL
I didn't know how…

(JANELLE interrupts him.)

JANELLE
I never would have cooked the stuff if I knew you didn't like it.

(Janelle executes several perfect lunges as she talks, which Paul finds distracting.)

PAUL

Do you have to do that?

(She ignores him.)

PAUL

Janelle. Please. You asked me to talk. Let's talk.

(She stops briefly, then resumes.)

JANELLE

I am talking.

PAUL

You're exercising.

(She continues lunging.)

JANELLE

I am exercising and talking. At the same time. It's called multitasking.

PAUL

It's distracting.

JANELLE

Only to those who can't.

PAUL

What does that mean?

(She stops lunging, takes a seat next to him on the couch.)

                        JANELLE

Nothing. You want to talk, let's talk. Let's talk about the
kale and why you lied.

                         PAUL

I wouldn't call it a lie.

                        JANELLE

What would you call it? For the past three years, every
single anniversary I have cooked Bobby Flay's mouthwatering…

(Paul makes a face at "mouthwatering." Janelle notices.)

                        JANELLE

His extremely mouthwatering recipe for Garlic-seared
Red Russian kale and cannellini beans. Every single…

(Paul interrupts.)

                         PAUL

Beans? I thought it was pasta.

                        JANELLE

We're gluten-free, Paul. We don't eat pasta.

                         PAUL

I thought maybe…on our anniversary.

                        JANELLE

No.

(SILENCE as Janelle realizes something.)

Wait. Do you mean to tell me you never once tasted it?

In three years, you never even once tried it?

                    PAUL
That first year I did. It made me gag.

(Janelle flashes him a look.)

                    PAUL
I'm sorry. It was stringy and bouncy and disgusting.
Like eating rubber cement...

                    JANELLE
(Incredulous.)

You've eaten rubber cement??

                    PAUL
...pickled rubber cement.

                    JANELLE
(Starts laughing.)

Pickled rubber cement?

                    PAUL
It was horrible. The most horrible thing I ever tasted. In
my entire life. And I am old, Janelle. Really old.

                    JANELLE
No argument here.

(Janelle gets off the couch and does several squats.
Throughout the following exchange, she squats, lunges,
does quad stretches)

JANELLE

You do know Red Russian kale is a delicacy, don't you?
An heirloom strain. It's not stringy or bouncy or anything, and if you hadn't lied to me about being a superfood aficionado, you'd know that. I bet you don't even
like quinoa.

PAUL

Of course, I like quinoa.

JANELLE

Hah. If you like quinoa, tell me what it is.

(Paul's been caught. He hasn't a clue.)

JANELLE

And how about acai?

(She waits half a second.)

You don't know what this is either. Do you?

PAUL

Could we go back to the kale? Please.

JANELLE

This isn't about kale, Paul. This is about lying. Your lying.

PAUL

I didn't lie.

JANELLE

You did.

PAUL

I spared your feelings.

JANELLE

My feelings? About kale?

PAUL

Yes. About kale. It's disgusting.

JANELLE

How can you say that? It's how we met.

PAUL

Doesn't change the fact that kale is an abomination.

JANELLE

An abomination?

(Paul is on a roll.)

PAUL

Against nature. A complete abomination.

JANELLE

That's silly. And kind of mean. We bonded over kale. Don't you remember? Whole Foods? Good Friday? It was raining? You rammed your cart into me.

PAUL

Other way around. You rammed your cart into me. The back of my knees. I nearly went down.

JANELLE

No, I didn't.

PAUL

Yes, you did. You left a bruise the size of an eggplant.

JANELLE

No.

PAUL

A small eggplant.

JANELLE

You have it all wrong. I...

(Paul interrupts.)

PAUL

You had salmon in your cart. It was wrapped in butcher paper. Fresh—probably organic—wild Pacific salmon. Eight ounces. I could read the label. You spent $17.57. On salmon. I figured you were rich—or crazy—to spend that kind of money on fish.

(Although Janelle doesn't stop exercising, she slows down, staring at Paul in awe.)

JANELLE

You remember all that? Even the price?

(Paul doesn't seem to hear the question.)

PAUL

And I wondered if it was the salmon that made you so damn strong you nearly knocked a grown man to his knees.

JANELLE

(More to herself.)

I had no idea. I thought you'd forgotten.

PAUL

You were wearing exercise clothes, remember? Tight exercise clothes. Like you always wear. Blue, I think. Maybe black.

JANELLE

Not black.

PAUL

Then blue. You were at the meat counter and you weren't watching where you were going. You turned your cart too fast and it hit me. You apologized. Profusely. I thought you were the cutest thing I'd ever seen. With your messy hair and tight clothes.

(Janelle is now completely engrossed in Paul's memories and stops exercising.)

JANELLE

And you were wearing shorts. And sandals. Birkenstocks. It was raining out, maybe 50 degrees and you're dressed for summer. I made you out to be some sort of alpha male trying to prove you never get cold.

PAUL

Or wet.

JANELLE

Or wet.

PAUL

I followed you to the produce section.

JANELLE

You wouldn't shut up.

PAUL

I was falling in love.

JANELLE

More like lust.

PAUL

Maybe.

JANELLE

That soon in, no maybe about it.

PAUL

Okay.

JANELLE

(Fondly.)

You just kept blathering on and on about superfoods and how you liked superfoods before anyone even called them superfoods.

PAUL

I'd read an article. JAMA, I think.

JANELLE

And how your favorite superfood was kale, but not just any kale. Red Russian kale.

PAUL

I wanted to impress you.

JANELLE

To get in my pants?

PAUL

Crude.

JANELLE

But accurate?

PAUL

Accurate.

JANELLE

Do you know hard it is to find Red Russian kale?

PAUL

I wanted to impress you.

JANELLE

But once we got married? You could have told me.

PAUL

When? That first anniversary, you were so excited about cooking that stupid...

JANELLE

Garlic-seared Red Russian kale. An heirloom variety, Paul. Almost impossible to find.

(Janelle returns to her exercising, but halfheartedly.)

JANELLE

I special ordered it. Had it shipped in fresh. On ice. Every anniversary. For three years. You could have told me.

PAUL

How?

JANELLE

And what did you even do with it?

PAUL

Threw it away.

JANELLE

Year after year?

(Paul hangs his head sheepishly.)

(Janelle stops exercising. Something has occurred to her.)

JANELLE

I bet you're not even gluten-free. Are you?

PAUL

Around you, I am.

JANELLE

All I ever wanted was for you to be healthy.

PAUL

I'm healthy.

JANELLE

You smoke cigars.

PAUL

Not a lot.

(Beat.)

JANELLE

You have high cholesterol.

PAUL

Not that high.

JANELLE

Same with your triglycerides.

PAUL

Come on, Janelle. For a man my age…

JANELLE

(Interrupting.)

You don't exercise.

PAUL

Not like you. Nobody exercises like…

JANELLE

(Interrupting.)

You're going to die and then I'll be alone.

PAUL

I'm not going to die.

JANELLE

Everyone dies.

PAUL

Not for a long time.

(Paul gets up, tries to wrap his arms around Janelle. She shrugs him off.)

JANELLE

Do you have any idea how long it took to find someone like you?

PAUL

Someone like me?

JANELLE

You. To find you. Do you have any idea how long it took? I'd never find someone again. Someone who wears shorts in winter, socks with Birkenstocks. Someone who laughs at my jokes.

(Beat.)

Most of the time. Someone who touches me just the way I need to be touched. Someone who loves me. I mean, really, Paul. I'm not easy to love. You know?

(Paul's not walking into that.)

JANELLE

I'm opinionated and crabby. I don't like people disagreeing with me, not at all. And I'm completely obsessed with my body.

                    PAUL
I am, too.

(Janelle smiles.)

                  JANELLE
I just don't want you to die, you know?

                    PAUL
I'm not going to die.

                  JANELLE
You will. You eat like crap.

                    PAUL
I don't eat like crap.

                  JANELLE
And you smoke cigars.

                    PAUL
Not that many.

                  JANELLE
And you don't exercise.

                    PAUL
I'll exercise.

                  JANELLE
Really?

(Paul realizes what he's gotten himself into. He counters with:)

PAUL

I'll eat better.

JANELLE

And quit cigars?

PAUL

I'll eat quinoa.

JANELLE

And quit cigars?

PAUL

I'll try that acai stuff.

JANELLE

And quit cigars?

PAUL

How about gluten? I'll give that up. Even away from you.

(Janelle considers this.)

JANELLE

And kale? Will you start eating kale?

PAUL

Only if you want me to die.

(Janelle reacts. She likes this.)

JANELLE

You'd do that for me? Eat kale and die?

PAUL

If that's what it takes.

JANELLE

You never know. It just might.

(Janelle performs one final, perfect lunge, then crosses to Paul. They hug.)

JANELLE

You know, you're not half bad.

(Beat.)

For an anti-kaler.

LIGHTS FADE.

The Great Kale–Cauliflower War

Chris Allen

No one was sure how the animosity began. Was it the article in *National Plantography* that compared the nutritional content of kale versus cauliflower? Was it the study that showed cauliflower was the more versatile vegetable? Was it kale's jealousy of cauliflower's constant appearance in alternative food products?

Whatever the underlying cause for the unrest between kale and cauliflower, the precipitating moment was etched in the annals of history. It was the day cauliflower showed up in a kale salad.

It had been an unseasonably warm day in April. Curly Kale was resting against the side of the bowl. Several of his friends lounged nearby, including Annie Arugula, a young, svelte leaf, her spiciness just blossoming, whom he had met at an organic food conference.

Suddenly, a shrill voice pierced the air, "What on God's green acre is that?"

"What's what?" Curly asked, molding his body to the curvature of the oiled wood side.

"That," Annie responded, pointing one of her lobed leaves at a bleached white stalk standing among a sea of green.

Curly leapt to attention, his edges fluttering in indignation. "That's a cauliflower. What on earth is he doing in a green salad?" His ruffles now blurred in fury. "Out damn vegetable!" Curly shouted. "You cannot be here."

Behind him, kale, arugula, and romaine lettuce spread out to the left and right. Everyone tittered and chattered at the disruption of the serenity of the salad.

The young sprout fell backwards, stunned at the aggression before him. "But I need to fulfill my destiny," he protested. "Someone left me out of a vegetable dish. I need to be part of your medley."

"Out," Curly commanded. "This salad is strictly for green leaves. Out, you albino apparition."

Spurred by the booming voice of their leader, the phalanx of leaves advanced on the hapless stalk, whose bulbous inflorescence was now quivering in fear. Retreating with a mighty leap, he sprang over the edge of the salad bowl. Curly rushed over just in time to see the small stem bounce off the counter and land, bruised and battered, on the floor where a dog cruising the kitchen mouthed him and then spat him out. Not quite the destiny the naïve cauliflower was hoping for, but one that satisfied the Kale Commander.

That intrusion upon kale territory, so innocent from the cauliflower's perspective, was seared upon Curly's memory. The episode had greatly upset his new friend, Annie, and it became the tipping point. He had enough. The House of Cauliflower's ascendancy threatened to usurp his power in the plant world and diminish the reputation he had carefully cultivated across scientific studies and social media. He called together a war council and thus began the historic Kale-Cauliflower War.

In a secluded corner of a grocery wholesaler's cool room, Curly sat at the head of the table, shuffling papers. Annie, enamored of Curly's stature, or to state it more obviously, she had a crush on him, observed from behind a row of celery. As the greenery gathered, Curly stood, unfolding to his full height. "We must crush the House of Cauliflower. They have encroached upon our territory, and it is time we put them in their place."

The House of Kale was substantial and had branches across the world. "We stand ready to defend you," proclaimed Lacinato (Dino) Kale.

"As do we," Premier Kale announced, hopping up to bang his stem upon the table.

"If it please you, sir," shouted the heads of the families of Siberian Kale, Redbor Kale, and Red Russian Kale, "we are also here to assist."

"Thank you." Curly nodded his assent. Turning to his left, he thundered, "Now, what say you Walking Stick Kale and Kamome Red Kale?"

The two remaining families had shunned the spotlight and were less well known than their more popular cousins. They were hesitant to become fodder for Curly's ambitions, but family pressure being what it is, Kamome stepped forward and said, "Um, OK, but do we really have to fight?"

Curly's stentorian voice reverberated across the room. "Of that, you may be sure. You will fight."

The assembled leaves shuddered.

The House of Cauliflower, in response to the rumors of the aggression of Kale, amassed its own army. At a little-known organic co-op on the south side of Venice Beach, four major families, Italian, Northern European annuals, Northwest European biennials, and Asian, appeared before the Great and Wonderful Ruler, Kaul-e-flower. Kaul was usually nonaggressive and preferred to be eclipsed by the more colorful vegetables in the plant world. The families wondered what he would say.

"I have called you all together to mark a sad day in the chronicle of our lives," Kaul began. "One of our own, a

71

young sprout with enormous potential, innocently tried to join a green salad. He was crushed, crushed, mind you, after being hounded out of a perfectly acceptable salad bowl. The perpetrator of this deed, the instigator of this mindless death, was none other than that arrogant collection of parenchyma cells, Curly Kale."

The normally passive stems, blanching stark white at the news, assembled around Kaul. Angry sputters roiled through the crowd. Finally, a shout, in unison, "We are here for you." The chorus was deafening. "Here to do your bidding."

The first battle began in early spring on a newly seeded cornfield in northern Nebraska. Neither side being well-versed in the strategies of war, the two opponents advanced to within proximity, rattling forks and knives. From a safe distance, since neither side wanted to get hurt, they hurled insults at each other.

The Kale side fired first. "Don't get too steamed, you stupid vegetable. You'll turn to mush."

The Cauliflowers responded, "If you skinny leaves turn sideways, no one will see you."

"Faux rice!"

"Ignorant garnish!"

This went on for hours until both sides, exhausted and not gaining any ground, retreated to rethink their strategies.

"We may have to employ weapons," Curly surmised. "Cauliflower is proving to be more stubborn than I had thought."

Annie rushed to his side. "My dear Curly. I fear this is all my fault. That day. In the salad bowl. I had never seen a cauliflower stalk before, and it scared me." She took a deep breath, gazed up at Curly, and implored,

"Please stop. This is not worth it. I don't want to see you injured."

The Kale Commander curled about his newfound friend. "My dear, this is war. Defense of honor! If need be, we will fight to the death."

Annie shrank back, uncertain of what had happened to the frond she had come to love. Something had taken hold of Curly, and she feared the consequences.

The next battle saw the two sides fully engaged, again pounding their knives and forks upon the ground, jeering and taunting. One eager kale sprig, over-inspired by Curly's rhetoric, lowered his fork and charged at the front line of Cauliflower, spearing a young soldier who was trying to blow into a bugle.

The clatter was deafening as the two sides engaged, knives and forks ready to impale anyone in their way. Pieces of kale and cauliflower shot off in every direction. By the time retreat sounded, and the weary fighters trudged home to their camps, the battlefield looked like a Vitamix® had spun through.

"We need a stronger weapon," Lacinto (Dino) Kale pounded on Curly's desk. "Something that will halt the House of Cauliflower in its tracks."

"Maybe we should just stop," Ornamental Kale sniffed, preening her frilly, purple and red leaves. "We have so much beauty to give to the world. We can't do it chopped and wilted, can we?"

"She's right," Annie urged, stroking Curly's ruffles. "Why can't we all get along?"

Curly brushed her off. "We must do this. We cannot lose our position on the politically correct food list."

The assembled branch leaders nodded and murmured in assent. Redbor stepped forward. "We need something that will humble Cauliflower, knock them back down to the unremarkable vegetable status they deserve."

"I have a culinary genius on my staff," Chinese Kale said. "He'll come up with something."

A few days later, the two sides lined up again, this time with knives and forks pointing directly at each other. Cauliflower's platoons advanced first.

"Not yet," Chinese Kale warned. "Not yet." It was important to hold all fire until the exact moment.

The Kale army waited until Kaul-e-flower's troops were within a few yards. Then a volley of onion slurry, heavily seasoned with jalapeno chile powder, arched from behind Kale's lines to thoroughly coat the Cauliflower foot soldiers.

Screams of anguish echoed across the field as the unfortunate front line abruptly reversed, trampling their fellow stalks as they retreated into a nearby forest of tomato plants.

The cheers and whoops of the Kale army resounded across the fields.

"We have won the day," Curly announced. "That will teach them."

"But, I fear, my dear love," Annie sobbed. "This is not the end."

Unbeknownst to Curly, Kaul-e-flower had recruited Broccoli as an ally. Strong, very green, and with a reputation tied to a former U.S. President, Broccoli had invented a secret weapon to use against Kale.

A few days later, Kaul-e-flower sent a message to Curly, stating his demands:

1. Kale will immediately cease all aggression.
2. Kale will admit Cauliflower makes a dandy pizza crust.

3. Kale will admit it is no longer the darling of the healthy eating world.

Curly read the missive and slammed it to the ground. "Of all the impudence," he roared. "This upstart will pay and pay dearly!"

"No, Curly, no." The Commander failed to hear Annie's protestations as tears fell from her face.

A week later, the Kale army had once again filled its tankers with the onion slurry and prepared to advance upon the opposing camp. In the lead were the special forces branches of their strongest allies: Iceberg lettuce, ready to bowl over and flatten Kaul-e-flower's tents; Romaine lettuce, tall and broad, ordered to envelope any head of cauliflower it saw; and Spinach, whose many baby leaves, slick with olive oil, would entangle and bring down the top-heavy foot soldiers.

Curly strutted back and forth in front of his impressive army. The sheer number of participants was intimidating. "Today will go down in history. Today you will fight for the supremacy of green leaves. Other leaves, at home, in their beds, will wish they were here on this momentous day."

Curly turned toward the battlefield. "Now, go get them."

The ground shook as Curly's forces rumbled down the slope. Shouting and yelling, the leaves, urged to a frenzy, waved and fluttered in a breeze of their own making. One hundred yards, fifty yards, the day was surely theirs.

Then, without warning, Broccoli unleashed his secret weapon. Darkening the skies, boiling through the air, came a thick cheddar cheese sauce. It plopped down from the heavens, thoroughly coating every leaf in sight.

So great was the weight of the sauce, the brigade

halted in its tracks.

As the Kale army struggled to move under the weight of the yellow sludge, Kaul-e-flower's troops, ecstatic at their success, jeered their doused opponents.

Then, an unexpected vision appeared. Rolling in from the east side of the field was a dazzling white hard-boiled egg. Riding atop was Annie Arugula, holding a skewer crowned by a white round of Daikon radish, the universal symbol of truce.

"Listen to me," she cried. "You don't have to do this. This is wrong." Her clear voice rang out, capturing the attention of the two commanders.

Curly made his way through his wounded soldiers to stare at Annie.

Kaul stepped out in front of his warriors. "Who is this?" he asked.

Annie urged the egg forward, stopping only when she was before both leaders. She glanced over at Curly. "I love you. But what has happened to you?"

She looked over at Kaul. "And you. How could you do this to your family?"

Both Curly and Kaul harrumphed, with Kaul adding, "Who is this upstart, and why is she interfering with our battle?"

Curly stared at the young shoot, sitting tall and straight upon her egg. "This slip of a leaf is Annie Arugula." His countenance softened. "I believe she is speaking truth to power." He strode toward her and announced, "Annie is my girlfriend. At least...." He gently touched one of her deeply indented lobes. "I'd be honored if she were my girlfriend. Perhaps we should hear what she has to say."

Annie dismounted and pulled a sheaf of papers from her backpack. "I've done research on *Plancestry*. We're all related. We're all cruciferous vegetables, one big, happy Brassicaceae family.

"Really?" Curly was skeptical.

Kaul said, "My grandfather told me I was related to Brussels sprouts, bok choy, and cabbage. Is that true?"

"Yes," Annie laughed. "Our family is huge, filled with stems and leaves."

Curly embraced his bright, brave Arugula. Enfolding her in a ruffle, he extended an edge of his leaf to Kaul. "Can we make peace?"

"Can you handle our differences? No matter what, we will still make better pizza crust and fake rice."

"I know," Curly said, taking two steps forward with his edge still extended. "And we will always be a better decoration for plated food, and taste better in sandwiches. We are different, and yet we are the same."

Kaul took the proffered edge. Clasping it within his inflorescence, he shook it heartily. "Let there be peace."

Cheers erupted from everywhere as leaves and stems embraced each other.

Annie beamed as she hugged Curly.

And, so ended the Great Kale-Cauliflower War.

The Kale Killer

Walter Walkow

It was 9:59 a.m. and Detective Waclaw Wywiadowca was sitting at his desk having his second cup of coffee when his phone rang.

"Hey, Law (that's what everyone called him, since no one could pronounce his name), it's Sergeant Flynn. I'm down here at the Sunset Arms Apartments responding to a call from the hotel manager about a disturbance in one of his tenant's apartments. We found a deceased male and based on the condition of the body, it looks like a possible homicide. Something's really strange."

"So, what's so strange?"

After a brief pause, Flynn responded. "You have to see this for yourself. I can't explain it."

Law put down his cup, grabbed his coat and walked to the desk of his partner, Jim Bueller. "Jim, we've got a possible homicide at the Sunset Arms."

"Homicide? We haven't had one in a while. This is basically a college town. I'll get my coat."

It was not a long drive to the apartment complex that housed many of the college staff. The two detectives met Sgt. Flynn at the entrance. Law shook Flynn's hand. "OK, what have we got?"

Flynn pointed inside. "Take a look for yourself, I can't explain it."

When Jim and Law entered the apartment, they saw a white, middle aged male sitting on the kitchen floor. He was propped against a cabinet. A strange, green substance protruded from his mouth and nose. Traces of blood stained his face.

Sgt. Flynn came over to Law.

"His valuables are intact and based on the broken furniture, there was a struggle. There are no signs of wounds to the body, just some blood around the face. Neighbors heard shouting and lots of noise, reported it to the apartment manager, who then called the station."

Law looked closely at the green material stuffed in the mouth. "What the hell is that? It looks like some sort of green plant." He bent down to sniff it. "Doesn't smell much, I hope forensics can tell us what it is. In the meantime, we need to find out who this is and get statements from the manager and neighbors."

He looked at Jim. "You talk to the neighbors while I find out more about this guy from the manager."

Flynn interrupted Law. "Based on the ID in his wallet, he's Robert Roses, a professor at the university. I told the manager to remain in his office in case we want to talk to him later."

Law thanked Flynn and reminded him to secure the crime scene.

While Jim contacted neighbors, Law headed for the manager's office. He could see the man was clearly shaken, his skin ashen, and his manner fidgety.

"What can you tell me about Robert Roses?"

"Not much to tell, kept to himself. Quiet, not many visitors that I ever saw. He wasn't around that much. Seems like he was always at the college."

Law tried to calm the manager. "Thanks. If you can think of anything else, call me. Here's my card."

Law met up with Jim in the parking lot. "So, what have you got?"

"The lady next door heard shouting, loud noises like furniture being knocked over, and then nothing. That's when she called the manager. She didn't know the tenant. Only saw him briefly when he left or came back. He wasn't very sociable."

"Not much here either. We should let the crime scene team gather any evidence and wait for the forensics report."

A few minutes later the crime scene team and coroner arrived. The detectives briefed the investigators, and then left.

Forensics delivered its report a few days later. Law read it, then walked over to Jim's desk. "The report says the likely cause of death was suffocation and the mysterious green stuff was kale. Based on the volume of it in the mouth and nose, it appears the kale was compacted tightly, cutting off any air. There were no fingerprints other than the victim's in the apartment."

Jim looked at Law. "You know, when I was a kid my father forced me to eat my vegetables, but this is going too far."

Both laughed at the dark humor.

"The newspapers are going to have a field day with this," Law smirked.

"Yeah," remarked Jim. "So, what do we know about this Robert Roses?"

"Forty-four years old, a biology professor at the college for the last fifteen years. Didn't have much contact with other members of the faculty—basically a loner. Has no relatives that we could find. Parents died ten years ago. Right now, we have no clues as to why someone would want to kill him. However, they must have been angry to do the thing with the green stuff."

"You mean with kale?"

"Yeah, whatever you call it."

A week later, Law got another call. It was from the police at the university. A female student, Mary Kleinmundt, age 22, was found dead by her roommate. Green plant material had been stuffed up her nose and mouth.

Jim and Law went to the student dorm to interview the victim's roommate, Judy Wong. Law started the interrogation. "When did you last see Mary?"

"On Friday afternoon, just before I took off for the weekend to see my folks," she sobbed.

Law continued. "Did she have any enemies or a boyfriend?"

"Her boyfriend's a Marine and deployed in the Middle East. I don't know about any enemies; I just got to room with her this semester. She wasn't from around here, and she seemed like a sweet person."

Judy pointed to her now-dead friend. "What's that green mess in her mouth?"

Jim answered, "That's kale."

Judy cringed.

The detectives waited for the crime scene investigators and coroner, and then left.

News travelled fast, and by the next morning, the local newspaper plastered a disturbing headline: *Kale Killer at Large.*

Forensics confirmed the green plant material was kale and the student died of suffocation. Interviews by Law and Jim at the college found no connection between the professor and the student. No fingerprints were found in the dormitory room, but there were signs of a struggle.

Back at the station, Law pounded on his desk, frustrated by the lack of progress on the case. "So far the only connection is the murder weapon—let's focus on the kale. The crime scene report noted that in both cases no kale was found on the victim's premises, so the perpetrator must have brought it. Let's have a lab test the kale and see if there is something unique about the samples."

The kale from both bodies was sent to a lab for analysis and to look for possible DNA left behind by the killer.

A week later, the Kale Killer struck again. This time it was Harry Winchell, a male, aged fifty. He was a journalist with the local newspaper. His housekeeper found him.

News of a Kale Killer spread nationwide. Kale sales plummeted as people were afraid to buy it, fearful they might be next.

Law enforcement faced pressure from the mayor and the public to solve the case. The police captain assigned detectives to interview chain grocery store managers, hoping to identify someone who bought large quantities of kale. Unfortunately, that effort did not bear fruit. The murderer could have purchased the kale from many stores. It was popular in the college town.

Finally, law enforcement got a break. Law reviewed the lab tests of the kale. "I think we have something here," he told Jim. "It seems all the kale we sent for testing share the same DNA. They also found the samples had the same mineral content. It's possible they came from the same source. We need to find that source."

Jim offered, "I'll get some other staff to go out to the grocery stores and get their sources of kale. Hopefully there won't be that many."

"Great, I will get someone to gather a list of farms in the vicinity that grow kale. Then we can match them to your list."

A few days later, Jim and Law compared the data about the stores and farms.

"What have you got, Jim?"

"You won't believe this, but we lucked out. They all use the same farm as their source. It's Happy Earth Farm just outside of town."

Law pounded his fist. "Bingo! I think, it's time to visit them."

Happy Earth Farm, owned by a local family, had been growing kale for two generations. The son, Jeff, whose parents started the farm, now ran the operation with his wife and their two children. He greeted Law and Jim when they arrived.

"Welcome. I'm Jeff and this is my wife, Jane. What can we do for you? Need some kale?"

Law responded, "No, I'm Detective Wywiadowca and this is Detective Bueller, my partner. We need to ask you some questions about your kale."

"Detective what?" asked Jeff.

"It's Polish," Law responded. "Never mind the name. We're here to get information about your kale."

"I bet you're here about the Kale Killer, aren't you? Just awful."

Jane turned to Law. "Kale is wonderful. Why would

anyone want to use it to kill?"

Jim nodded his head. "Well, that's what we want to know, too. We have information that the kale used by the killer might have come from your farm. Has anyone other than your typical grocery store customers come here to buy kale?"

"No, not that I'm aware of. Both my wife and I are usually here and would know about that."

Law interjected, "Is it just you and your wife and kids that run the farm?"

"Pretty much, though we do have a hired hand, Jake Matthews, who helps with the harvest. He lives in the small cabin next to the main house."

"Is he here now?' We'd like to talk to him."

"No, today's his day off."

"Well, we need a sample of your kale to take back with us."

Jeff directed Law and Jim to a batch of kale that had been prepared for sale. "Here take as much as you want. It's not going anywhere. With all the publicity about kale…well, sales are in the tank. We may have to move to another crop to survive and, in the meantime, lay off our hired hand. We're not harvesting it anymore."

"Do you folks know a Robert Roses, Mary Klein-mundt, or Harry Winchell?" Law inquired.

Jeff and Jane looked at each other, eyebrows raised, shaking their heads. "No, never heard of them," Jeff responded.

"Well, thank you for your time. We appreciate it." Law extended his hand to Jeff. "When is your worker, Jake, coming back, in case we need to talk to him?"

"He's due back tomorrow."

On the drive back to the office, the detectives compared notes about the visit.

"Jim, I want to get the kale from the farm tested to see if it matches the kale from the killings. I suspect we will find it does. It's possible the killer got kale from a source far from here, but my instinct says it came from this farm."

Offering a thumbs-up, Jim responded, "I think you're right on that, though I don't think Jeff or his family are involved. They have a very secluded life and I see no connection to either Mary, Robert, or Harry. Besides, I doubt they would use kale as a murder weapon. Remember what they said? 'Kale is wonderful.'"

"Yeah, right." snickered Law. "But I am curious about the farm hand, Jake. We need to talk to him. While we're waiting for the test results on this kale, I think we need to re-examine the possible links among the deceased. All they have in common is kale. Why? Isn't that the question we need to answer?"

"Yeah," Jim snorted. "Kale's the murder weapon, weird as that is. That's the common thread, so far. We just don't know *why*. If the lab tests confirm the murder weapon is kale from Happy Earth Farm, we need to get back and talk to Jake."

Law added, "You know, if we can find a link to kale, we might have our motive. Hope it isn't a serial killer who selects random victims."

Back at the office, Law wrote on the whiteboard:
- Money / Possessions—Who profits? Who gets what?
- Anger / Revenge—Who is angry and why? Who did what and to whom?

He turned to Jim. "Maybe it's the killer's relation to

kale that we need to uncover. Why kale? Is the killer angry at kale for some reason?"

Jim rolled his eyes.

Law continued, "Suffocating the victim with kale is definitely a sign of anger. But why is it directed at these *specific* individuals? And are there more?"

Jim responded, "I certainly hope not." What about money?"

"I don't think money is the motive."

"Why not?"

"Come on, Jim. How much money can you make on kale?"

"So that leaves anger or revenge. Or both."

"I think so." Law looked smug, as he crossed his arms over his chest. "I'll trace the biology professor's connection to kale. You do the same for the journalist. Whoever is done first can do the student."

"OK, Law, sounds like a plan."

The next day, storming over to Jim's desk, Law announced, "I think I have a connection for the professor. Seems Robert Roses promoted the health benefits of kale three years ago, focusing on it as a treatment for cancer."

Jim, who had been working all night, responded. "I got something similar with the journalist. He wrote a series of articles about a woman who died of cancer after experimental kale treatments failed. There was a lawsuit against the college and Professor Rose, and the journalist sided with the judge's decision to dismiss the suit as frivolous. I looked up the case and it was initiated by the son of the woman who died from the treatments. His name is Peter Small. Seems he was really angry. After the proceedings, he disappeared. That was almost five years ago."

"Great work," Law commended. "I learned Judy Wong recently published a paper that recommended examining kale again as a treatment for cancer. By the way, the lab tests came today and confirmed the kale from the farm matches our samples from the killings. Now that we have a motive and the source for the kale, we need the killer. Let's get a warrant to search the farm. And definitely interview Jake."

"It's coming together," Jim smiled.

Law leaned his cheek on his fist. "Jake would have had access to the kale. He hasn't been at the farm very long. Let's see if he's who he says he is." He thumped his hand on the desk. "Get photos of Peter Small and Jake Matthews from the state's motor vehicle division."

"Just what I was thinking," Jim said, as he leaned back in his chair and grinned. "If the photos match, then we'll have enough evidence to convince a judge to issue a search warrant on Jake Matthews, or whoever he is."

Later that afternoon, Jim received an email containing the photos he requested. He quickly turned to Law. "Take a look, pal."

Law gave a low whistle.

"They're the same person," Law chuckled.

Jim added. "And he had the opportunity—access to the kale grown on the farm. I'll go see the judge, explain what we have, and get a search warrant."

He returned about an hour later, waving a paper in his hand. "OK, I've got the warrant. Let's go."

When they pulled into the gravel parking of the farm, Jake was standing by his car, near his cabin.

88

"Jake Matthews," Law addressed him, "or should I say Peter Small...we have a warrant to search your cabin, your car, and your belongings."

Jake squinted his eyes and screwed up his face. "What are you talking about...Peter Small? I'm Jake Matthews."

Jim got nose-to-nose with Jake and looked him directly in the eye. "Give it up; we have your photos from Motor Vehicles."

Jake's shoulders slumped and his whole body deflated.

Law turned to Jim. "Take him in the cabin. Meanwhile, I'll search the trunk."

"Well, what do we have here?" Law said to a large stash of glistening kale stashed in a cardboard box in the back of the trunk." He joined Jim in the cabin.

"What did you plan to do with all the kale in your trunk?" he demanded of Jake.

But Jake remained silent.

Jim continued to guard Jake while Law explored the cabin. He found spoons and screw drivers that had traces of green material and what he was sure looked like dried blood. Newspapers strewn on a sofa and kitchen were open to Harry Winchell's newspaper articles about a lawsuit and the death of a woman who relied on kale for her cancer treatment.

Law yelled to Jim from the other room in the cabin. "I found newspapers related to the cancer case."

Jake bolted for the door, but Jim quickly grabbed him. "Where do you think you're going?"

Law joined them from the other room and addressed Jake. "Jake Matthews, alias Peter Small, I arrest you for the murders of Robert Roses, Mary Kleinmundt, and

Harry Winchell."

Jim handcuffed Jake, read him his Miranda rights, and seated him in the back of the car for the ride back to the station. Within an hour, Jake's full interrogation commenced. When faced with the evidence found at the farm, it didn't take long for him to confess.

After Jake was taken to a jail cell, Law turned to his partner. "You see, it just confirms no one is beyond the reach of the Law."

Jim rolled his eyes. "Humble, aren't you?

A trial was held later that year. Peter Small, alias Jake Matthews, was convicted of three counts of first-degree murder and was sentenced to three consecutive life sentences in a prison.

One of the main foods served at the prison was kale.

Project Resurrect and Illuminate Kale – Memo 7

TO: Bella
FROM: Eric
RE: PRIK, Week 7

To be honest, Bella, PRIK is struggling, but we continue to push the kale envelope.

- Team Chemistry thought they had hit the big one when they developed a kale paste to combat toenail fungus. Unfortunately, they learned toenail fungus loves the kale's nutrients. It mushroomed in size and spread throughout their building. A hazmat team has been called to clear the area, but they have advised the space will be unusable for the next six months. The team had to move to temporary office space. The office manager made us pay in advance.

- Team Cuisine has been hard at work devising new recipes. Since raw in salads, stewed in stews, and dried in chips are already out there, it is really testing their mettle to create something new. They tried shaping kale into pseudo beef patties, fake chicken nuggets, and molded salmon. To date, these products have been upchucked by our panel of tasters. The cleaning crew refuses to enter that lab after hours. They say they need a fifty percent raise in salary before they will engage in removing the green slime and odious stench resulting from the testing.

I am convinced we will crack this ribbed kale leaf. We continue to persevere.

Eric

Milk was once good for you...before anyone heard of kale.

Kale—Super Food? Or Super Gross?

Maureen Cooke

We've all heard it: when it comes to superfoods, kale is one you shouldn't live without. Mix it in your smoothie. Throw it in your salad. Even sauté it with a little garlic and olive oil. But whatever you do, do not fail to include this all-purpose, nutrient-rich wonder food in your daily diet.

And what if you just can't stand kale? What if the taste leaves you gagging? What then?

Well, could be your genes. Could be you're what's known as a PTC taster, meaning you have a gene that enables you to discern a bitter flavor in kale.

And what does *that* mean?

Turns out that kale, like other cruciferous vegetables, such as Brussel sprouts and spinach, is high in a substance known as phenylthiocarbamide, which, for some, tastes nauseatingly bitter. For others, kale and Brussel sprouts are no big deal.

Turns out that being a PTC taster could be a beneficial evolutionary adaptation. According to the Genetic Science Learning Center at the University of Utah, the ability to perceive a bitterness in foods, such as kale, prevented early humans from eating poisonous plants. Check out the Learning Center's web page (https://learn.genetics.utah.edu/content/basics/ptc/) for a more thorough discussion.

And what if you're not a PTC taster, yet, for whatever reason, you're simply not a huge fan of kale and would prefer if it never crossed your lips?

Easy. Don't buy it.

But what if you're at a party and your host, or hostess, serves a kale salad? Or sautéed kale? Or a kale smoothie? Or even kale chips?

Well, how's your thyroid? How's your ability to lie about your thyroid? According to several popular websites, including *WebMD*, people with hypothyroidism should limit their intake of kale and other cruciferous vegetables, as they can interfere with thyroid function.

The caution regarding cruciferous vegetables stems from research on rabbits with syphilis in 1928. According to Canadian nutritionist Alina Petre's article, "Are Goitrogens in Foods Harmful?" https://www.health-line.com/nutrition/goitrogens-in-foods) scientists discovered that rabbits developed goiters and resulting loss of thyroid function when fed high amounts of cruciferous vegetables.

More recently, endocrinologists, such as Dr. John Morris of the Mayo Clinic, argue that, unless you have an iodine deficiency (quite rare in the United States), a moderate amount of cruciferous vegetables, including kale, won't hurt you.

However, if you want to get out of eating kale, reference that 1928 study. If nothing else, your host, or hostess, is bound to be impressed with your choice of reading material.

Finally, lately there has been a tendency for pet owners to share their food, especially their superfoods, with their dogs. When it comes to kale, don't.

Although the website nomnom.now (https://www.nomnomnow.com/blog/kale-is-a-superfood-for-dogs) characterizes kale as a superfood for dogs, other websites, including that of the Massachusetts ASPCA (https://www.mspca.org/), explain that kale can cause gastric distress. In addition, it is high in calcium oxalate, which can cause kidney and bladder stones.

So, go ahead, enjoy your kale. Just keep it away from your dog.

Project Resurrect and Illuminate Kale – Memo 8

TO: Bella
FROM: Eric
RE: PRIK, Week 8

Bella, this morning I pulled into the parking lot and was accosted by a hulking beast of a man who called himself Jim and claimed to be a former Navy pilot. It seems he has a passionate hatred for kale. He heard about PRIK and was determined to stop any efforts to increase the use of kale in this world.

After hearing his arguments and seeing the size of his beefy arms wrapped around my throat, it came to me. I don't like kale either. Therefore:

I QUIT!

Good luck with Cameron Nash. Jim and I are going out for lunch at a certified kale-free restaurant.

Eric

Recipes

A Word about Recipes

As we have all heard, kale is considered a superfood, loaded with necessary components for the efficient functioning of the human body. It contains more calcium, Vitamin K, and Vitamin A than almost any other whole food. And it contains a lot of iron. Its strong green color hints at the copious amounts of goodness found packaged within its often-ruffled leaves. There is no denying it. Sitting in the produce section, nestled with lettuce, endive, and arugula, it stands out, trumpeting, "I am good for you!"

You've seen kale everywhere in the supermarket. In smoothies, as chips, added to pasta dishes, soups, and stews.

There is no end to its uses. This section contains a collection of recipes, all about kale. One is the creation of noted chef, Jane Butel. Some are original concoctions developed for this anthology. Some are adaptations of existing recipes.

While most are quite delicious, the reader should beware. Read the ingredients and methodology carefully. Like kale itself, one or two of these recipes might not be what they seem.

And, of course, if you're an anti-kaler, you are good to go without trying a thing.

Chris Allen

Slivered Kale Salad with Roasted Winter Vegetables and Spicy Orange Sesame Dressing

Jane Butel

With the sudden interest in anything kale, I decided to try some fresh kale salads and found that shredding the kale very finely—similar to the way you cut cabbage for cole slaw works best. High heat roasted carrots, beets and onions add a wonderful taste treat, especially when dressed with the spicy orange dressing and the salad is scattered with toasted sesame seeds.

Yield: 4 servings

Ingredients
2 medium sized beets
2 carrots
1 onion, quartered
1 tablespoon olive oil
1 teaspoon sea salt
3 cups slivered kale
2 tablespoons toasted sesame seeds
Orange sesame dressing

Method
1. Preheat oven to 450°F. Rinse the vegetables, then place them on a cookie sheet and drizzle with the olive oil and sprinkle with the sea salt.

2. Roast for 15 minutes and check the onion and carrot by piercing with a fork—if soft remove from oven to a cutting board. Continue roasting the beets until tender—about 30 more minutes.

(Roasting the vegetables can be done early in the day or up to a week ahead.) Chop the onion and carrot. Peel the beets and chop.

3. To serve, prepare the salad dressing in the bottom of the salad bowl or in a separate bowl. (see below) Then add the kale, roasted vegetables, toasted sesame seeds, and a few grinds of black pepper. Toss with the dressing and serve.

SPICY ORANGE SESAME DRESSING

This is good on winter salads made with dried fruit or most salads served with pork, poultry or seafood.

Ingredients
½ cup extra virgin olive oil
3 tablespoons freshly squeezed orange juice
1 teaspoon orange zest
2 teaspoons freshly squeezed lemon juice
½ teaspoon minced habanero chile
1 teaspoon Dijon mustard

Method
1. Whisk all ingredients together until foamy and toss with the salad.

Colcannon

Adapted from the Irish by Sandi Cathcart

Yield: 4-5 servings

Ingredients

4 cups dreaded kale (or more depending on how many potatoes you use), sliced thin, stems removed (original recipe calls for green cabbage)
6 green onions or to taste, sliced
Garlic to taste
Red potatoes, cut into pieces
Salt
Pepper
Garlic powder, optional
Hidden Valley® Ranch dressing dry packet, (about 1-2 oz)
Unsalted butter
Milk

Method
1. Sauté kale, onions and garlic in small amount of olive oil until wilted and tender. Set aside.

2. Cook potatoes in water until tender. Mash with spices and dressing.

3. Add dreaded kale mixture.

Commentary
Can be made ahead and reheated in microwave.

Kiki's Kale Salad

Adapted by Sandi Hoover

Yield: 6 Servings

<u>Ingredients</u>
Dino Kale, approx. two bunches
A good vinaigrette dressing (Braggs® is yummy, but your choice)
¼ cup dried cranberries
1 sweet potato
3 tablespoons pumpkin seeds
3 tablespoons toasted sunflower seeds
½ cup toasted pecan pieces

<u>Method</u>
1. Bake sweet potato (30-45 mins at 425 degrees, depending on size), let cool. If done the day ahead, store in refrigerator overnight.

2. Remove stems/tough veins from kale and slice into strips.

3. Add small amount of dressing to kale and massage it into the leaves until coated. This softens the kale and marinates it in the dressing without drowning it. Add more as necessary. Better when kept in the fridge overnight. Add more dressing and massage again if it seems dry.

4. Cube sweet potato and add to bowl of marinated kale.

5. Add cranberries, seeds and nuts just before serving to keep the crunchy things crunchy.

6. Serve cool or at room temperature.

Surprise Green Smoothie

Sandi Hoover

Yield: 2 servings

Ingredients
2 cups Dino Kale, stems removed, roughly chopped
1 cup crushed pineapple in juice
1 orange, juiced
1 banana
ice cubes
(½ cup cold water, optional)
1-3 mint leaves

Method
1. Place fruits and kale in blender
2. Add ice cubes or water
3. Blend
4. Add more ice cubes if necessary
5. Blend until desired consistency is reached
6. Enjoy immediately

Adrienne's Kale Pie
Adapted from urbandreamer.org

Yield: 8 -10 Servings

I make this pie in a round casserole—13 inches across and 3 inches deep. It's much bigger than a pie plate! This would make two standard large pies and you may have filling left over.

Ingredients

Crust
3 cups flour
½ cup butter, cold
1 cup shortening, cold
1 tablespoon sugar
½ teaspoon salt
10-14 tablespoons ice water

Method
Make the crust:
1. Combine flour, butter, shortening, sugar, and salt in a bowl using two butter knives or a pastry blender until the butter and shortening are the size of small peas.
2. Add ice water. Form into a ball. If it's too dry to form a ball, add ice water, one tablespoon at a time, until it does.
3. Knead the ball 4-5 times and then cover and refrigerate for about 15 minutes.
4. When ready, remove from fridge, divide in two, and roll each into a circle large enough to fit your

pan with an inch or inch and a half hanging over the side.

5. Grease the pan and put the bottom crust in very gently without stretching the dough.

Filling

2 pounds kale, or a mix of kale, Swiss chard, beet greens, and/or escarole. At least half of the mix should be kale. Clean, blanch (cook 4 minutes in salted boiling water), drain, dry, then chop.
1 tablespoon olive oil
2 tablespoons butter
1 shallot, minced
1 clove garlic, minced
1½ cups shredded cheese: mozzarella or a mix of mozzarella and parmesan
1 cup cubed fresh mozzarella
1 cup ricotta cheese, drained
1 pound sausages, fully cooked and sliced
4 whole eggs plus 1 egg yolk
½ pound sweet potatoes, peeled and chopped
½ cup heavy cream
Salt and pepper to taste
An additional egg, to glaze the pie crust.

Make the filling:

1. Chop the sausage and sweet potatoes and spread on a cookie sheet. Drizzle with a tablespoon of olive oil and shake the pan to coat. Season with a teaspoon of salt. Bake at 350 for 20 minutes or 'til the sweet potatoes are softened.

2. Melt the oil and butter at medium heat in a large sauté pan. Sauté the shallot and garlic until soft. Add the greens and cook until they are soft and the liquid is mostly evaporated.

3. Meanwhile, combine the eggs, cheeses, cream, salt, and pepper in a large bowl. Add in sausage mixture, greens mixture, and mix gently until combined.

<u>Bring it all together:</u>
1. Put the filling in the bottom crust.
2. Lay the top crust over everything and cut vents in it.
3. Whisk an egg with a teaspoon of water and brush the top crust.
4. Bake at 350 degrees for 1 hour. I put the pan on a cookie sheet to catch any dripping juices.

Kale *des Ordures* – a "Down the Hatch" Kale Recipe

Jim Tritten

Editor's note: Read this recipe through to the end before attempting to make it.

Yield: 1 serving

Ingredients
1 pound Siberian kale (Common Curly kale if not available)
1 Limoneira brand lemon
2 tablespoons organic Hazelnut oil (Culinary Moroccan Argan Oil by Dip & Scoop oil if not available)
1 small Cipollini onion (also known as Italian spring onion)
⅕ clove Bogatyr or Metechi garlic
Pinch of dried hot double-cut red pepper flakes
1 tablespoon *Laurent du Clos* red-wine vinegar
¼ teaspoon Pink Himalayan salt

Method
1. Cut stems, veins, and center ribs from kale. Discard.

2. Cut kale into ¼-inch wide strips along the length of the leaves. Makes about 8 cups.

3. Squeeze juice from lemon into small bowl.

4. Halve the onion lengthwise and then thinly slice crosswise.

5. Mince the garlic.

6. Gently massage kale leaves with lemon juice and a spritz of hazelnut oil. Set aside in a bowl and let stand for five minutes. Repeat process two or three times until leaves are flexible and do not crackle when bent.

7. Bring a 6-quart pot of salted water to a rapid boil, slowly add kale, leave the pot uncovered while stirring counterclockwise slowly so as to not damage the leaves.

8. Check to see when the leaves are tender but not wilted (roughly ten minutes). Drain into a ceramic colander and let cool.

9. Using a 12-inch cast iron skillet, heat oil on medium-high without smoking the oil. Add and sauté onion, stirring counterclockwise, until onion starts to caramelize (roughly six to eight minutes). Add the garlic and red pepper flakes. Stir slowly. When garlic fragrance becomes pronounced (roughly one minute), reduce heat to medium and add the kale. Continue to stir slowly while leaves cook to dark green. Remove from heat, add vinegar and salt, and let cool.

10. Pat leaves dry with paper towels and place them in a bowl.

11. Drain off oils from skillet into a container and set aside. Return skillet to stove, add one pound of maple-flavored bacon, and cook to taste.

12. As the bacon is cooking, add three tablespoons of organic coconut oil to bowl containing kale leaves. Stir clockwise again careful not to damage the leaves. Carry the bowl to garbage, tilt, and allow contents of bowl to slowly slide into the receptacle.

Cover garbage receptacle.

13. Remove bacon from skillet and serve. Leftover oils in liquid container can be used to rejuvenate scalp and nourish hair.

Kale Farewell

We hope you enjoyed *Kale is a Four-Letter Word* and would love to hear from you.

Our email address is: corraleswritinggroupllc@gmail.com

Better yet, leave us a review on Amazon. A good one, of course, unless you want a truck emptying its entire load of kale at your front door.

Editors,
Patricia Walkow and Chris Allen

Whether you eat kale or not, you're going to die.

THE CORRALES
WRITING GROUP

Photo by Jasmine Tritten, LLC

Members of the Corrales Writing Group who contributed to this anthology. From the left, then around the table: Patricia Walkow, Sandi Hoover, Maureen Cooke, Jim Tritten, and Chris Allen.

The Corrales Writing Group was established in 2012 to provide a comfortable setting for a group of authors to write and receive critiques of their work in a supportive environment. The writers have the opportunity to submit pieces every two weeks. Other members respond by indicating what is working, what is confusing, is there any repetition of words and thoughts, and finally by identifying what the work is about vs what the story may want to be about. The author is always in control of their product and can revise or not as they evaluate the input.

Members of the group engage in ongoing education to improve their writing. They attend workshops, classes, and writing conferences, and some of them have been presenters at these events. The organization has also provided information to other groups as to how to conduct a successful critique group and how to publish their work.

Since 2013, the Corrales Writing Group has published five anthologies of short stories and their e-book equivalents. These publications have received numerous awards at the state and national level as well as outstanding reviews. Individual members' stories, articles, and books have also been published nationally and internationally. Many of these works have received awards as well.

Members contributing to the anthology are shown above. New members are Peter Gooch and Joe Brown.

PATRICIA WALKOW
Corrales Writing Group
Member, Contributor, and
Lead Editor

Photo by KateThePhotographer

Patricia Walkow is an award-winning author and editor. She wrote an acclaimed biography, *The War Within, the Story of Josef,* which received first place honors both nationally and internationally. Ms. Walkow has contributed to many anthologies and edited several. Her editing work and short stories have been recognized for excellence, either at the state or national level. A member of the Corrales Writing Group and SouthWest Writers, her work appears regularly in print and online anthologies, newspapers, and magazines.

CHRIS ALLEN and Ember
Corrales Writing Group
Member, Contributor, and
Co-Editor

Photo by Paul Knight

Chris Allen lives in Corrales, NM, with her botanist/ artist husband, Paul Knight, and lots of farm animals. A retired archaeologist, she enjoys writing humorous stories inspired by her chaotic life as a community volunteer, an extra in film productions, a fiber enthusiast/ sheep breeder, and an equestrian. A member of the National Federation of Press Women and New Mexico Press Women, her work has received awards at the state and national level. She is currently collaborating on two other books, a romance mystery with fellow Corrales Writing Group author, Patricia Walkow, and a science fiction novel with Paul. Chris can be reached at christina.g.allen@gmail.com.

JANE BUTEL
Guest Contributor - Recipe

Photo by Steve Larese

Jane Butel is internationally recognized for popularizing Southwestern food and is the author of thirty-two cookbooks. She operates a non-vocational cooking school and Pecos Valley Spice Co., a web based source for pure Southwestern ingredients.

SANDI CATHCART
Guest Contributor - Recipe

Photo by John Cathcart

Sandi Cathcart was born in Alaska and grew up in the South Pacific, Asia, and Africa. For twenty years she and her Air Force husband lived in Europe, numerous states, and South America. They have two children and two grandchildren. In 2015 they retired to South Carolina and live with a rescue dog, four feral cats, and two elderly parents.

MAUREEN COOKE
Corrales Writing Group
Member, Contributor

Maureen Cooke is a versatile writer with an M.A. in English, who studied with John Nichols (*Milagro Beanfield War*), Rudy Anaya (*Bless Me Ultima*), Harry Lawton (*Willy Boy*), and Matthew McDuffie (*A Cool, Dry Place*). Her work has appeared in college journals, California newspapers, and *Baby Talk*. Her fiction has been honored with fellowships at the University of California, Riverside and the University of New Mexico. She lives in Corrales with her menagerie of animals.

ADRIENNE EVATT

Guest Contributor - Recipe

Photo Courtesy Adrienne Evatt

Adrienne Evatt is the owner/operator of Urban Dreamer Farm & Vineyard in Auburn, California. A retired twenty-plus-year corporate executive from a Fortune 5 company, Adrienne now spends her time with her husband and daughters, baking dozens of pies, cakes, cookies, and croissants for her weekly farm stand. Her cookbook, *The Urban Dreamer Cookbook*, will be self-published in 2020. Adrienne is a self-taught chef, inspired by her passion for food and lifetime of travel.

SANDI HOOVER
Corrales Writing Group
Managing Member,
Contributor

Photo by Richard Hoover

Sandi Hoover is fascinated by the natural world. This led to her career as executive director of the Houston Audubon Society and the Bayou Preservation Association, active conservation non-profits. Her writing was focused—no humor or fiction in position papers and environmental statements. The Corrales Writing Group has afforded a helpful place to grow as an author.

ALEX KNIGHT
Guest Contributor – Art Work

Photo Frank Frost Photography

Alex Knight is an actor and visual artist living in Los Angeles, California. He was born in Albuquerque and raised in Corrales, New Mexico, which he still calls home.

PAUL KNIGHT
Guest Contributor – Art Work

Photo by Chris Allen

Paul Knight has worked as a botanist and artist for over forty years. His work displays different aspects of animals and nature as captured in jewelry, watercolors and sculpture. Color and detail are evident in his paintings while his sculptures capture movement and shape. His earrings, pendants and bracelets display the form and whimsy of the natural world. Paul has published numerous technical articles throughout his career, and he is currently working on a science fiction novel with his wife, Chris Allen.

JASMINE TRITTEN
Guest Contributor – Prose; Art
Work as Jasmine Tritten, LLC

Photo by Jim Tritten

Jasmine Tritten is an artist and writer born in Denmark. Jasmine has written numerous short stories that have been published in various anthologies. Her memoir, *The Journey of an Adventuresome Dane* published in 2015, won an award. She wrote a children's story with her husband and made the illustrations. *Kato's Grand Adventure* was published in July 2018 and won five awards. Jasmine resides in enchanting Corrales, New Mexico with her husband and four cats.

JIM TRITTEN
Corrales Writing Group
Member, Contributor

Photo by Jasmine Tritten, LLC

Jim Tritten retired after a forty-four-year career with the Department of Defense including duty as a carrier-based naval aviator. He holds advanced degrees from the University of Southern California and formerly served as a faculty member and National Security Affairs department chair at the Naval Postgraduate School. Dr. Tritten's publications have won him forty-two writing awards, including the Alfred Thayer Mahan Award from the Navy League of the U.S. He has published six books and over three hundred chapters, short stories, essays, articles, and government technical reports. Jim was a frequent speaker at many military, arms control, and international conferences and has seen his work translated into Russian, French, Spanish, and Portuguese. He lives in Corrales, NM with his Danish author/artist wife and four cats.

Photo by Patricia Walkow

WALTER WALKOW
Guest Contributor – Prose

Walter Walkow is a solutions architect in the data sciences group at Sandia National Laboratories, a Department of Energy Research laboratory located on Kirtland Air Force base in New Mexico. While most of his literary work has been of a technical subject matter, he has been a contributing author to the Corrales Writing group. As a child immigrant from his native country, Germany, English is a second language. His wife often reminds him when his syntax is distinctly foreign. Life is not tranquil living with an active dog, a cat, and an ambitious author wife, but it seems right living in the village of Corrales. You may contact him via email at walkoww@earthlink.net

Illustration and Photo Credits
In order of appearance

Maria Svyryd/Shutterstock

Cory Thorman/Shutterstock

Rawpixel.com/Shutterstock

Denise Torres/Shutterstock
This image is used as a
header in each PRIK memo.

Mr. Rashad/Shutterstock

Toltemara /Shuttterstock
and
Daria Chegaieva/Shutterstock

Farbled/Shutterstock

Jasmine Tritten, LLC

This image is used as a text
separator throughout the book.

Alex Knight

Serlin Sehii/Shutterstock

Lukasz Siekerski/Shutterstock

Jasmine Tritten, LLC

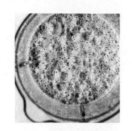 Rawpixel.com/Shutterstock

 sirtravelalot/Shutterstock

 Dundanim/Shutterstock

 Jasmine Tritten, LLC

 Tashnatasha/Shutterstock

 rumsde/Shutterstock

Jasmine Tritten, LLC

3DDock/Shutterstock

Banc Rouge/Shutterstock

Lightspring/Shutterstock

Paul Knight

Paul Knight

Paul Knight

Milk image by Unknown
Author, licensed under
CC BY-NC
Kale image by Patricia Walkow

Gilles Lougassi/Shutterstock

Daria Chegaieva/Shutterstock

Patricia Walkow
Kale for sale at Albertson's

Patricia Walkow
A menu item from The Range Café in
Albuquerque, New Mexico.

Patricia Walkow
Kale & Cheese Ravioli from Sprouts
market.

Patricia Walkow
Cracker Barrel® Brussel Sprouts 'n
Kale Salad.

Jasmine Tritten, LLC

Patricia Walkow
A bunch of kale at Albertsons.

Jasmine Tritten, LLC